INITIATION

Other books in the
CANTERWOOD CREST SERIES:

CANTERWOOD
CREST

INITIATION

JESSICA BURKHART

ALADDIN M!X

New York London Toronto Sydney New Delhi

This book is a work of fiction. Any references to historical events, real people, or real locales are used fictitiously. Other names, characters, places, and incidents are the product of the author's imagination, and any resemblance to actual events or locales or persons, living or dead, is entirely coincidental.

m!x

ALADDIN M!X

Simon & Schuster Children's Publishing Division

1230 Avenue of the Americas, New York, NY 10020

First Aladdin M!X edition January 2012

Copyright © 2012 by Jessica Burkhart

All rights reserved, including the right of reproduction
in whole or in part in any form.

ALADDIN is a trademark of Simon & Schuster, Inc., and related logo
is a registered trademark of Simon & Schuster, Inc.

ALADDIN M!X and related logo are registered trademarks
of Simon & Schuster, Inc.

For information about special discounts for bulk purchases,
please contact Simon & Schuster Special Sales
at 1-866-506-1949 or business@simonandschuster.com.

The Simon & Schuster Speakers Bureau can bring authors to your live event.
For more information or to book an event contact
the Simon & Schuster Speakers Bureau at 1-866-248-3049
or visit our website at www.simonspeakers.com.

Designed by Jessica Handelman

The text of this book was set in Venetian 301 BT.

Manufactured in the United States of America 0620 OFF

10 9

Library of Congress Control Number 2011940168

ISBN 978-1-4424-1948-3

ISBN 978-1-4424-1949-0 (eBook)

*To Drew for being the first guy cool enough
to e-mail me and say you're reading Canterwood.
Keep reading and being exactly who you are.* ☺
*I hope you like the character named after you,
as promised!*

ACKNOWLEDGMENTS

Thank you to everyone at Simon & Schuster, especially those who have been initiated: Fiona Simpson, Bethany Buck, Mara Anastas, Dawn Ryan, Carolyn Swerdloff, Craig Adams, Jessica Handelman, Nicole Russo, Russell Gordon, Karin Paprocki, Lucille Rettino, Courtney Sanks, Alyson Heller, Deane Norton, Virginia Herrick, the fantastic sales team including Mary Marotta, Jim Conlin, Christina Pecorale, and the countless other people who support Canterwood.

Thank you, Stephanie Voros, for working so hard on the rights for the series.

Thanks to the fantastic models, stylists, makeup artists, and to Monica Stevenson.

Special thanks to the bookstores and employees who have introduced Canterwood to readers.

Jill Cikowski, thank you for being a part of Team Canterwood! Horse Mystique board members, you all are THE BEST. Big ♥s for the support and love you've shown to Kate and me! The GET WELL SOON banner you created for Kate, among other things, we'll never forget.

Brianna Ahern, your texts and kitty pics got me through some rough spots. Thank you for being there at all hours. Lauren's blog was your idea—thank you! Hug A for me!

Lauren Barnholdt, you're a constant source of support.

Thank you, Katherine Devendorf, for being the world's best Jane of all trades: managing editor, cat sitter, and kitty photographer.

Alex Penfold, the offers of a home-cooked meal were so sweet, as were the flowers from you and Paula Wiseman. Thank you both.

Thanks to Becca Leach, Kelly Krysten, Jennifer Rummel, Mandy Morgan, James Booth, Carrie Ryan, and April Aragam for the encouraging Tweets.

Josephine Piraneo, thank you for keeping the Canterwood Crest website looking so lovely.

Joey Carson, thank you for offering business advice and being a wonderful new friend. Hugs to Lexi and Grace!

Ross Angelella, I loved our late-night UES write-a-thons. We got some *serious* work done.

Shout-outs to the music/TV that I used for inspiration while writing this book: *Pretty Little Liars, Switched at*

Birth, *The Nine Lives of Chloe King*, *The Glee Project*, *The Voice*, Lady Gaga, 2am Club, Andrew Belle, and Keane, among others. Find my complete *Initiation* playlist on my blog.

Julia Reed at Sakura of America, thank you for offering Gelly Roll® pens for a contest. The prizes are greatly appreciated!

Thank you, Hana Johnson, for providing Pro Hair Tinsel in a variety of colors as a giveaway during the book's release. I heart Hair Flairs!

Kate Angelella, Canterwood is a fifty-fifty product cultivated by both of us. You are not only a wickedly talented editor, but also an author, a business owner, and the best friend a girl could hope for. I'm honored to co-own Violet & Ruby with you. I'm so excited to see what the future holds. My wish came true when you came to the dark side and started writing full-time. I remind myself every day how lucky I am to have you in my life as more than just my BFF. LYSM. ♥

1

LAUREN TOWERS,
INSOMNIAC

11:59 p.m.: Days left: 1!

Tomorrow morning (!) I leave home and Briar Creek for Canterwood Crest Academy. I got up to blog because I could not sleep. Usually, I'm up late on Fridays anyway, but not like this. Blogging is better than talking sometimes because I can sit down and let all of my thoughts come out unfiltered on the page. I've been blogging all summer—Dad's suggestion—and now I'm totally addicted to it.

I'm scared about tomorrow. So scared. I'm still second-guessing all of my decisions about everything. I'll admit it: All of these questions keep rolling around my brain, like:

Am I leaving Briar Creek too soon?

Am I ready for the competitive riding life again?

Are Whisper and I prepared?

Will anyone find out my secret before I'm ready to talk about it or any other part of my past?

That last question is the one keeping me awake. Tonight and every night.

Posted by Lauren Towers

2

MY SIDE

THIS WAS *REALLY* IT.

My breath caught, forcing me to sit on the bare twin bed. My parents and older sister, Becca, had dropped me off in my new dorm room only an hour ago.

I already had eight light blue sticky notes lined up along my eggshell-colored walls. At least I knew I was still *me* at Canterwood—the crazy-organized, to-do—list compulsive girl that my friends liked to tease.

I stared at all the boxes with *Lauren* scrawled on each in grape Sharpie. My roommate hadn't arrived yet, so I'd picked the right side of the room, hoping she wouldn't mind.

This was surreal. I—Lauren Towers—was a seventh grader at Canterwood Crest Academy—one of the most elite boarding schools on the East Coast. The Connecticut school had a reputation for rigorous academics and—the main reason I'd applied—an even more intense equestrian program. I picked up my BlackBerry and scrolled through my photos. There were a few family pics of Mom, Dad, Becca, and Charlotte—my oldest sister.

I tightened my grip on my phone's sky-blue gel case when a photo popped up of me with my best friends, Brielle and Ana. In the picture, the three of us were smiling at the camera as we posed on horseback. We were—*had been*, I corrected myself—riders at Briar Creek Stable. Even though it was summer in the photo, my skin was as porcelain pale as it was now in the fall. Sunlight glinted off Cricket, the Welsh cob school pony that I'd ridden at Briar Creek.

I put my phone down—unable to continue looking at the pictures. They would only make me miss everyone and everything. I surveyed my room, my boxes. Mom, Dad, and Becca had helped me move in a *ton* of luggage, duffel bags, and boxes. I imagined how it would look with my poster and my laptop. Right now, the room was empty. Once it was decorated, it would look amazing. I could tell already.

Gentle September sunlight streamed through two large curtainless windows. I couldn't wait to decorate with

my roommate. My room at home had a light-blue-and-white color scheme. Light, sky-blue was my favorite color and decorating was one of my favorite things to do. I'd brought a messenger bag of pages and pages that I'd torn from design magazines for inspiration.

I lived and breathed for fashion, decorating, and riding. Hopefully, my roommate would like some of my ideas. The last thing I wanted was for us to clash on day one.

Khloe Kinsella. I said her name to myself. My guidance counselor and math teacher, Ms. Utz, had given me and Khloe each other's e-mail addresses so we could determine who would bring what for our room. I'd started a "what to bring to CC" list in a purple-with-silver-polka-dots notebook.

I'd e-mailed Khloe first just to say hi. Her reply was friendly enough, but she seemed really busy. She'd e-mailed sporadically throughout the summer and had given me just enough information to know what to bring to school. We hadn't exchanged much personal information. My stomach churned a little at the thought of meeting the girl I'd be living with for the year.

I weighed options, flipping through the Canterwood campus guide I'd gotten in the mail weeks ago. I wanted to go to the stable to see my horse, Whisper. But I was

nervous about going to the stable alone. I'd been there with my parents and Becca to get Whisper settled. But everything had been so new and unfamiliar, I hadn't paid attention to anything but Whisper. It was as if I hadn't gone to the stable at all—I couldn't even remember much of what it looked like, let alone how to get there. It had been a whirlwind of activity around me. I *did* remember that Whisper had a giant, roomy box stall that she'd settled into quickly. And before I'd left, she'd taken a delicate sip of water from her pink bucket and started munching hay.

And okay, maybe there was . . . another reason I was stalling. Even though I *knew* no one recognized me—that no one paid attention to seventh graders—my nerves still wouldn't go away. The fear that someone at the stable would look at me sideways, squint for one second too long and wonder if maybe I was that girl from TV. I tried to shake the thoughts from my head. I didn't want to fixate on that.

Mom and Dad already spoke to Mr. Conner, I reminded myself. They'd already met with my riding instructor, Mr. Conner, and explained my background. He'd understood that I wanted to keep my past just that and had promised not to mention previous competition experience or

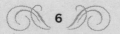

anything else that would connect me to what had happened. No one would find out anything from him—not one student on campus would know until—*if*—I ever decided to tell them myself.

I glanced out the window again, chewing the inside of my lip. I wanted to be with Whisper, but I wasn't ready to face the new stable yet. Just a little more time. Maybe some unpacking would distract me. I began to visualize where I wanted to put some of my belongings. I stood, surveying the layout of the room again. The double room was even bigger than I'd expected. There were two twin beds separated by space for two bedside tables. The windows above each bed looked over the gorgeous courtyard, which made the room feel even bigger.

On my side of the room, near the door, was a skinny counter with a microwave, two cabinets and space for the cheerful yellow mini-fridge that would be arriving any day from Pottery Barn Teen. Khloe and I had gone in on it together.

Each side of the room had its own closet with enough room on each side for one desk. I squinted my eyes. There was enough floor space for a small coffee table if Khloe and I decided we wanted one. I walked into the private bathroom on Khloe's side of the room. New white tile had been scrubbed clean, along with a shower with a glass door, a decent-size vanity mirror, and a wooden cabinet under the sink. I already had several ideas for color schemes in mind—I couldn't wait to talk about them with Khloe. We'd learned over e-mail that both sets of parents had given us "decorating allowances" to make the room feel like home.

I walked out of the bathroom, looking at my reflection in the full-length mirror. It had taken me almost all summer—*no* exaggeration!—to choose my first-day-at-Canterwood outfit.

Since it was Saturday, I'd decided to go for comfort-slash-chic. Skinny dark wash distressed jeans, a short-sleeve slouchy black tee with thin gray horizontal stripes, and a white tank underneath. For accessories, I'd decided on my beryl birthstone necklace. Classic and never out of style. I'd seen them on legendary icons from Audrey Hepburn to today's hottest celebs featured in *Trends* magazine.

I smoothed my long, wavy brown hair—letting the soft curls cascade down my back. My makeup was minimal—a sweep of shimmery caramel eye shadow that accented my blue eyes, concealer where needed, and a coat of CoverGirl's LipSlicks in Princess. Before we'd left home this morning, I'd applied a thin layer of Neutrogena

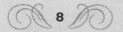

moisturizer with SPF 30. I never left the house without sunblock. Becca said my sunscreen obsession made me smell like summer all year round.

Footsteps stopped outside the door and a key turned in the lock. Khloe! My hand flew to my necklace—a beryl birthstone on a thin silver chain with a tiny diamond above it. Beryl stones were naturally clear, but my parents had gotten me one with a light blue tint.

The door opened and I clutched the blue stone tighter. A pretty girl with warm brown eyes stared at me. She was about my height, tan, and her long blond hair hung in beachy waves around her shoulders. She looked as if she'd come from California, not Boston, where she'd told me she lived. She looked *très* glam in a white tier-ruffled A-line skirt, a clover-green V-neck shirt, and a three-quarters-sleeve cardigan. Gucci sunglasses were perched on top of her head, and delicate silver bangles hung from her tiny wrists.

She dropped two purple faux-crocodile bags that she'd had slung over her shoulders, and they thudded to the floor.

She turned to face me, put her hands on her hips, and jutted out her chin. Her pearly pink lips pursed. "Well," Khloe said flatly. "I guess you've already chosen *my* side of the room."

3

DRAMA QUEEN
KHLOE

I CLASPED MY NECKLACE HARDER, MY MOUTH opening and shutting. *Great, job, Lauren,* I thought. My roommate knew me for ten seconds and she already hated me!

"I'm *so* sorry," I said, a flush spreading from my face to my neck. "I didn't mean to make that decision without you. It should have been something we talked about. I'm happy to change sides and—"

Khloe grinned, clapping her hands.

Okay, now I was *completely* confused.

"Yes! You totally bought it! I mean, unless you're acting, too. You're not, right?"

"Not *what*?" I asked.

Khloe put her hand over her mouth. "Oh, no. I scared you. I'm sorry, Lauren! I'm in Canterwood's drama program. I was just trying out my ubermean girl character. I've been working on her all summer."

I sat on my bed, breathing again.

"So . . . none of that was real?" I asked.

Khloe hurried over to sit beside me. "I'm serious—I was totally joking. I'm so sorry. I honestly didn't think my mean girl was any good. I thought you'd see right through *her*. I don't care what side of the room I'm on! Trust me. I wouldn't have even cared if you'd painted the room black before I'd gotten here."

I looked at Khloe. Sincerity radiated off of her. Regret and empathy filled her brown eyes.

I smiled—wanting her to feel better. She *had* been kidding.

"You *definitely* fooled me," I said. "I was ready to request a room transfer!"

Khloe smiled. "Is it wrong that what you said makes me feel bad and good at the same time?"

"No way," I said, laughing. "I never would have been able to pull that off the way you did. If I ever decide to take drama, I'll definitely have to come to you for advice."

Khloe kicked off her silver Havaianas, taking a seat on my bed. "I want to be an actress more than anything. Well, that and a professional equestrian. I know it sounds crazy, but I can *totally* do both. You said in your e-mails that you're a rider, too."

I nodded.

"What else are you into?"

"Well, I was in glee club at my old school," I said. "So, I'm definitely trying out for Canterwood's glee club. And, of course, I still have to test for the riding team to see where the instructor will place me."

Someone knocked on our door, still left partially open after Khloe's dramatic entrance. A tall, bald man stuck his head inside.

"Miss Kinsella?" he said.

"Right here," Khloe said, raising her hand and smiling.

"I've got the rest of your luggage," the man said. "I'll put it right inside."

"He's a mover my parents hired to help bring my stuff from home to Canterwood," Khloe explained.

From the hallway, he unloaded boxes and a few suit-cases onto Khloe's side of the room. She thanked him and he left the room.

Right away, I noticed that none of her boxes were labeled. Not even her name was anywhere. *I'd* been two seconds away from ordering a label maker, but Becca had talked me out of it.

"How do you know what's in each box?" I asked. "I practically went through a package of Sharpies labeling mine."

Khloe got off the bed, unzipping a zebra-print suitcase. "You'll find this out soon enough—I'm the most disorganized person *ever*." She scanned my boxes. "Wow. Maybe some of your organizational skills will rub off on me. Everyone knows I need it."

Khloe flipped open the suitcase's top, revealing riding boots in zipper cases, a couple of helmets—one with scrapes, that had to be for practice only—and the other in a cover, that I guessed was for showing. A half-dozen pairs of leather gloves and stock ties were in a knit bag in a side pocket of the suitcase.

"I swear," Khloe said. "My dressage stuff takes up half of my suitcases. I've got two filled with show coats, shirts, and breeches. And that doesn't even count the bags for my other riding stuff."

"You're a dressage rider, too? That's my favorite discipline!"

I couldn't believe how lucky I was—Khloe had learned my last name via e-mail, but still didn't know about my accident.

"Cool!" Khloe said. She unzipped another suitcase.

"My roommate last year, Isabella, wasn't a rider. She was sweet, but she got bored whenever I talked about horses."

I frowned. "That must have been frustrating. Did she switch roommates? Or . . ."

"Isabella transferred to another school. She tried, but she couldn't keep her grades up. She was put on academic probation and finally decided to leave. She didn't think she'd ever be able to make it here." Khloe sighed. "Or she just didn't want to."

That made my stomach a little rumbly. I hoped that everything I'd put into Yates Preparatory—my old school—would prepare me for Canterwood. Yates had been *hard*, but it hadn't been anything compared to the summer homework I'd done for Canterwood. I'd received e-mails from all of my teachers with books to read, terms to know, syllabi—my inbox had almost overflowed.

"I heard that both classes *and* riding are tough here," I said. "My riding team placement test is on Monday. What level are you?"

Khloe paused for half a second. "Advanced. I was intermediate my first year, though. Mr. Conner is really, really strict, but he's the *best* instructor. He teaches most of the intermediate and advanced classes."

Khloe pulled a pair of paddock boots from another

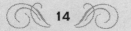

suitcase and rummaged through a giant hot-pink bag until she found a pair of jeans.

I thought about what she said—*advanced*. That used to be me. The girl on the fast circuit who competed at every possible show and never took a day off. Would Khloe ever know that girl?

"Oh! I'm going to the stable," Khloe said, pulling me out of my thoughts. "If you want to come, I'd love to give you a tour."

"You don't mind showing the newbie around?" I smiled. "Really?"

"It'll be fun. Plus, I want you to meet my horse and some people at the stable. Did you bring your own horse?"

An insta-smile took over my face. It always came whenever I thought about Whisper. "I did. My mare, Whisper. I just got her this summer, so we're still in that getting-to-know-each-other stage."

"That's an exciting place to be," Khloe cooed. "I've had my mare, Ever, for almost three years."

"I can't wait to meet her."

I got up, went straight to the plastic container labeled *shoes* and slid my pink-socked feet into my black Ariat zip-up paddock boots. I'd gotten the new boots for Canterwood and I loved how shiny and scuff-free they were.

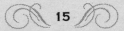

Khloe finished lacing up her paddock boots, shaking her head at me. "Okay, *maybe* I should have labeled a few boxes."

She shot a look of helplessness at her stack of luggage.

"We can help each other unpack," I said. "It'll be my thank-you for showing me around."

"Deal." Khloe smiled and I did, too. Just minutes ago, I thought I'd been assigned a nightmare roommate. Now, it felt as though Khloe and I could be friends. She wasn't like any of my old friends—she was outgoing and theatrical. Her personality would take some getting used to, but I looked forward to getting to know her better.

4
ACTING OUT

KHLOE OPENED OUR DOOR AND WE STEPPED into the hallway of our dorm, Hawthorne Hall. I *loved* Hawthorne—it was even more beautiful than the online pictures. I'd only stared at them every five seconds all summer long.

The building's three stories hosted only seventh-grade girls. Hawthorne was adjacent to Orchard Hall. The dorm where *Sasha Silver* lived. Sasha—the superstar rider who happened to have also trained at Briar Creek before I got there.

The eighth grader was a Briar Creek legend. Photos of her and her horse, Charm, practically wallpapered my old instructor's office. I wanted to ask Khloe if she knew about Sasha, but I wasn't ready to bring up anyone connected to my past. Not yet. Not until I was completely sure I could trust Khloe with . . . anything. Everything. Maybe even my secret.

Hawthorne's walls were soft yellow, making the place feel welcoming. Gleaming wooden floors had forest green carpet runners. A giant vase of vibrant orange dahlias decorated a long mahogany table near the office of Christina, the dorm monitor. The table had a stack of Canterwood handbooks, brochures on different electives, and course schedules. Green and gold pens (school colors) were in a GO CANTERWOOD! jar for students to take.

Lots of dorm room doors were open and girls were hugging each other. Almost every one said something like, "Omigod! I missed you this summer!" or "You got *so* tan over break!"

A few girls eyed me—a look I knew well. They were scoping out the new girl. I'd learned, as much as anyone could, not to be intimidated by that look. Instead, I smiled at them without batting an eye. Some even did the same back.

"Hey, Khlo!" a smiling girl called, as she rolled two suitcases down the hallway, expertly steering them around another girl's luggage.

"Lex, hey! Catch up after we get moved in and I'll introduce you to my new roomie?"

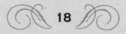

The girl—Lex—nodded, smiling at both of us. She had dulce de leche-colored skin and beautiful, curly black hair with reddish highlights that skimmed her shoulders. "Def."

Khloe and I walked the rest of the way down the hall. "I'll introduce you to everyone when we get back from the stable," Khloe promised. "Hawthorne looks big, but there aren't a ton of girls who live here—hopefully you won't feel too overwhelmed."

We opened the glass doors with HAWTHORNE HALL etched into them and walked down the pretty brick stairs, which were lined with iron railings.

Khloe looked at me for a second. "You know, you look pretty together for being the 'new girl,'" she said.

"I moved a lot," I explained. "Canterwood's my fourth school, so I'm kind of used to the whole 'new girl' thing."

"Ah," Khloe said as we walked along the winding side-walk, past park benches and old-fashioned streetlamps. The black lanterns had glass lamps and gas-lit flames. I couldn't wait to see them at night.

"This place is the most beautiful school I've ever been to, though," I said.

"So, why'd you move so much?" Khloe asked. "I've only been to two schools—my local public school and then I enrolled in Canterwood last year."

"You're from Boston, right?" I avoided her question. I was so annoyed at myself. How had I already brought up something connected to my secret? Especially a secret that could ruin my future at Canterwood if it came out before I was ready.

"Yep," Khloe said, answering my question and forgetting her earlier one. "I rode for a pretty good stable in Boston, but my parents and I thought a boarding school with an equestrian program would be better for me. And, *bonus*, Canterwood has riding *and* a fab theater program."

"Equestrian and actress—double threat," I said.

"Equestrian and glee club—also double threat," Khloe said, grinning.

We walked through an idyllic cobblestone courtyard. Benches circled a fountain and water streamed down a granite stone. I paused to read the quote on the stone.

Education is the best provision
for the journey to old age—Aristotle.

"See how academic crazy they are?" Khloe asked, waving an arm at the fountain. "Even *that's* serious about school."

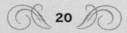

I laughed. "If I start to see quotes in the sidewalk then I'm bailing."

"You didn't answer my question before," Khloe said. "Do you have a parent in the military or something? Is that why you move so much?"

Just answer her, I told myself. I couldn't avoid her question.

"We moved if I found a stable that was better for my training and one where I could travel less. Family is big in my house."

Khloe nodded and I breathed a sigh of relief. Maybe acting was in my future, after all.

"That's really great experience—being at all of those stables. I've lived in Boston my whole life. But every year for my birthday, I beg my parents for one thing."

"What?"

Khloe flashed her had-to-be-Zoom!-whitened smile. "To move to Los Angeles so I could act."

"That would be quite the present," I said. "I'm guessing they always say no?"

"Yep! Totally ruined my life!" Khloe put a hand over her forehead, sighing. "How's my *dramatic* look?"

"Your sigh could have been longer," I teased.

Khloe nodded as if she was taking my advice seriously.

"Well, *maybe* they didn't ruin my life," Khloe said. "I love Boston and I'm not ready for L.A. Not *yet*. But after enough classes at Canterwood, I know I'll make it. I've been in every school play. I'm *so* excited because auditions for *Beauty and the Beast* are on Friday. I ran lines with my friends all summer for the part of Belle. It's *the* role of the play. I spent all of my allowance on voice lessons so I could sing."

"Auditions in the first week of school is intense," I said. "Can anyone watch?"

Khloe shook her head. "Anyone can try out, but auditions are closed. Why?"

"I hoped I could come and cheer you on."

"That's so sweet!" Khloe said, smiling. "Well . . . I bet I could sneak you into the back."

"I'm so there."

"Awesome! They're at seven," Khloe said. "We can go over together."

The smile stayed on her face. I was glad she wanted me there. Supporting her would be a good way to start off our friendship.

"And totally count me in to be there for your glee club audition," Khloe said. "I'll be waiting for you."

We passed the guidance building—I recognized it

from the student handbook. If I remembered the campus map right, the brick building meant we were close to the stable.

I couldn't stop questioning Khloe. Maybe because, to me, acting felt like an extension of glee.

"So, what do you want to do?" I asked. "Stage? Big screen? TV?"

"Soap operas. I've watched *Pretty in Port Royal* with my mom since I was in, like, second grade. All summer, I taped it and practiced my favorite character's lines— Skylar Storm."

Before I could reply, Khloe made a swooping motion with her arm. "And I give you the best stable in Connecticut."

5

UNDERSTUDY
NOT-SO-BUDDIES

WE STOPPED. UNLIKE THE FIRST TIME I'D
been here today, I took it all in. The black stable with
white trim was pristine. Numerous paddocks with dark
brown fences surrounded the stable. Dirt and grass arenas
fit like puzzle pieces near the stable.

Dressage markers were set up in one of the smaller
arenas and another had a jump course. Behind the stable,
a couple of guys took their horses through figure eights.

"There's another big arena off to the right side," Khloe
said, her eyes following my gaze. "Mr. Conner and his
two main stable hands, Mike and Doug, built a permanent
cross-country course on the other side of that hill."

There was so much more riding space here than at
Briar Creek. I didn't even know where I wanted to ride

first. I'd visited a lot of stables, but none of them even came close to this.

Khloe walked onto the gravel toward the entrance. The open giant double doors allowed a slight breeze to go through the stable.

When we stepped inside our boots tapped against the concrete. Horses stuck their heads out over their stall doors on both sides of us. Wooden tack trunks lined the aisle and gold name plates shone from every stall door. The stable buzzed with people—there was activity everywhere.

Horses were being led in and out of stalls, clipped to crossties, and put on a large hot walker in the stable's center.

This place was *très* amazing. I couldn't wait to tell Brielle and Ana all about it.

"Let me give you a quick tour," Khloe said. "If you've already explored and know where everything is, just say the word."

"I put my stuff in the tack room earlier," I said. "But I was kind of in a haze."

"Ah, yes—the first-day-of-Canterwood haze. Follow me."

Khloe took me to the stable's tack room, filled with rows of gleaming saddles and bridles. She pointed out

Mr. Conner's office and pushed open the door to a spacious bathroom so I could see inside. Khloe showed me the entrance to the hayloft that was forbidden to students but where "everyone went anyway to gossip," and the feed room.

"Want to meet Ever?" Khloe asked.

"Of course!"

Khloe led me toward the end of the aisle.

"Whisper's down here, too," I said. "I like this part of the stable—it's so quiet. I'm glad she's here since she's new."

"And keep in mind the stable's not always like this," Khloe said. "It's usually a lot calmer. Everyone's here at once because they're moving back in. This . . ." Khloe unlatched a stall door and motioned for me to follow her inside. ". . . is Ever."

"Oh, wow."

Khloe's mare was gorgeous.

The big bay mare's dark brown coat gleamed evidence of meticulous grooming. Her beautiful face had a star—the white stark against her coloring—and her black muzzle looked velvet soft. I reached out a hand.

"She's a Hanoverian," Khloe said. "And the sweetest." Khloe wrapped her arms around the mare's neck. Ever

leaned into Khloe, blowing out a breath of contentment. Their bond was evident. I couldn't wait until Whisper and I were that close. We were closer every day, but we weren't Khloe and Ever. Not yet.

The mare reached her muzzle toward my hand and I stroked her face. "I love her," I said. "I can tell how tight you guys are. She's in amazing shape, too."

The mare's muscles were taut and toned in all the right places. She had the look of a dressage horse.

"She's my baby," Khloe said, kissing the mare on the cheek. "I want to meet your horse."

We stepped out of the stall and turned toward Whisper's.

"KK!"

Khloe and I'd barely turned around before a girl with wavy red hair and blue eyes grabbed Khloe in a hug.

"Clare!" Khloe threw her arms around the other girl. They almost knocked each other over.

"Omigod, I missed you all summer!" Clare said, stepping back from Khloe. Her pale skin was accentuated by bright blue eyes. Her clothes, preppy-chic, had a fashionable flair. She'd put a heather-gray three-quarters sleeve cardigan over a plum-purple tank top. Her black leggings were tucked into tall boots. *Magnifique.*

"I missed you, too! Skype was sooo not enough. Oh,

Clare." Khloe reached over and pulled me toward them. "This is my new roomie, Lauren. She's a rider."

Clare shot me a smile. "Hey. Welcome to Canterwood."

"Thanks. I'm excited to be here. Khloe's been showing me around."

"Of course she has," Clare said, shooting a sideways look at Khloe. "You never know when the role of 'campus tour guide' will show up in the classifieds. Now Khloe's prepared for that part."

Khloe punched Clare's arm. "Oh, puh-lease!" She raised her index finger in the air. "First of all, you don't find acting gigs in the classifieds. That's what *Backstage* magazine is for. Second, I wouldn't need to practice for that. And as if *I'd* try out for 'tour guide.' When I start auditioning, it'll be for the role of a beautiful, young ingénue who falls in love with a guy she can't have and does anything she can to get him anyway."

Clare and I looked at each other—a grin passed between us at the dreamy look in Khloe's eyes.

"Um, come back from soap opera land to Canterwood, please," Clare said, waving her hand slowly in front of Khloe.

We all started giggling. I liked Clare, and if she was friends with Khloe, maybe we'd become friends, too.

"Clare!"

Clare, Khloe, and I turned as a petite Asian-American girl with long black hair in a French braid walked up to us.

"Riley!" Clare hugged the other girl. "When did you get here?!"

The girl smoothed her red and white striped, capped-sleeve shirt. "A few minutes ago. Mom forgot to set her alarm, shocker, so we left late."

Riley didn't hug Khloe. The girls exchanged smiles, but there was *something* . . . odd between them—I could feel it. The mood changed from bubbly to flat.

"Is Adonis in his stall?" Khloe asked, her tone light. "I'd love to see him."

Riley shook her head, shimmery light green eye shadow accenting her dark brown eyes. "He's being his difficult self about getting out of the trailer. Mr. Conner's unloading him—he told me to come and make sure his stall was ready."

Riley's eyes turned to me as if she'd noticed me for the first time. She looked me up and down.

Slowly.

"You must be new," Riley said.

"Oh, I'm so sorry, Lauren!" Khloe said. She smacked her forehead. "That was so rude. Riley, this is my new roommate, Lauren. Lauren, this is Riley Edwards."

She didn't introduce Riley as her friend, I noted.

"Hi," I said. "Nice to meet you."

Riley's eyes stayed on my face. It felt as though she was studying me. Sizing me up. Deciding if I was a possible friend, someone to ignore, or a potential enemy.

"I know we just met," she said, tilting her head. "But you're so familiar. I feel like I've seen you before."

Panicky beads of sweat formed on the small of my back. *Keep it together.* I scolded myself. *Riley could be mistaking you for anyone.*

Besides, it would be *très* arrogant to think she knew me from the show circuit. Just because Riley thought she'd seen me before didn't mean she knew who I was or anything about my . . . secret.

I forced myself to smile. "I've moved around a lot. Where are you from?"

"Maine," Riley said.

"I've never lived there," I said.

Riley stared again for what felt like *forever* before a tiny smile passed over her face. "Hmm. My bad."

She turned to Khloe. "Khloe, you hear about the auditions for *Beauty and the Beast*?"

Khloe straightened, pushing her shoulders back. "I got the notice from Mr. Barber over the summer. Practiced every day."

Riley smiled. "Me too. My parents got me an acting coach and I had lessons twice a day. I'm going out for Belle. I mean, I *did* get the lead in *Into the Woods* last year."

Clare shifted almost as if she was unsure who to stand closer to—Khloe or Riley. Khloe and Riley's eyes were locked. Both girls were smiling, but I'd been around enough competitors on the A-circuit to know what was going on.

This was Psyching-Out-the-Competition 101.

"You sure did," Khloe said. Her mouth smiled, but it didn't reach her eyes. "And you were great."

Riley put a hand over her heart. "Aw, thank you, Khlo. But remember, you were *so* close to getting the lead. Too bad I'm so healthy. As my understudy, you would have gotten a chance to be onstage if I'd gotten sick. Maybe next time! We'll see each other this Friday at auditions, right?"

Clare cleared her throat, giving Riley and Khloe a smile. "And I'll be in the wings silently cheering you on."

Riley shifted to lean against Ever's stall. "And Lauren, you've got a big day tomorrow. Omigosh, are you *so* nervous?"

"About what?" I asked. I wasn't going to let this girl scare me.

"Testing for the riding team. You *did* know about it, right?"

I nodded. "Of course, and—"

"Most riders practice all summer before they come here," Riley said, cutting me off. "And they barely make the beginner team."

"I'm glad I trained so hard, then," I said. "I'll just have to do my best and see what happens."

Riley nodded. "Anything *can* happen during testing. Advice?"

I wasn't going to turn her down. But that didn't mean I'd believe every word she said.

"Sure," I said cautiously. "I could use any tips you've got."

"I was so nervous at my testing last time," Riley said. "Mr. Conner is *super* nitpicky, he looks for any little mistake. I never get rattled, but I did during my testing at the most important part."

"What's that?" I asked.

"Jumping," Riley said.

It took every ounce of control I had not to drop to my knees.

I'd been working hard—so hard—since my secret accident. The one I couldn't even think about. The one

I couldn't even start to remember when I had so much to master at Canterwood. But Riley had shaken me with one word.

Jumping was how it had happened.

Stop thinking about it, I told myself. *Not in front of these girls. Not in front of my potential new teammates.*

"Oh," I said, keeping my cool. "I like jumping, but dressage is my specialty."

Riley gave me a tiny smile with a sour hint about it. "At Canterwood, *everything* better be your specialty."

Clare's eyes shifted between Riley and me like she wanted to save me. "Riles, let's go see if Adonis's stall is ready, 'kay?"

Riley nodded and gave Khloe and me a little wave. "Later." Riley paused, looking back over her shoulder. "And Khloe, can't wait for Friday."

The two girls disappeared down the aisle. I waited for Khloe to speak. I didn't want to be the one to say something wrong if I'd completely misjudged the dynamic.

"Ooomiiigod!" Khloe shrieked.

6

SWEET TREATS
(OF MANY VARIETIES)

I JUMPED, LOOKING AT HER. HER HAND WAS across her forehead. "She's trying to take over *everything*! Riding *and* acting."

"So . . . I'm guessing you and Riley aren't BFFs?"

Khloe leaned up against the stall door. "It's a really uncomfortable situation. *Clare* is my best friend and Riley is her other best friend. Riley and I have been competing against each other for years—everything is about mind games and winning for her. I've tried to put it aside for the sake of my friendship with Clare, but Riley's even competitive about that."

"That's too bad," I said. "Clare seemed so nice. And I can tell that Riley's a little . . . territorial."

Khloe rolled her eyes. "Don't let her psych you out—I

noticed that she didn't waste two seconds trying to scare you about tryouts."

"Is jumping really what I should focus on?"

"Riley *lied*. Everything's equally important to Mr. Conner," Khloe said. "I have no clue why she said jumping was so important, but she knows better."

Just hearing Khloe debunk Riley's advice about jumping being key slowed my racing heart. She was right— Riley was just trying to psych me out!

"Thanks, Khloe," I said. "So . . . you want to stop talking about someone you don't like and come meet Whisper?"

Khloe's eyes sparkled. *"Definitely."*

I shook Riley off with every step toward Whisper's stall. Once we were just steps away, the mare poked her head over the door.

Her brown eyes widened when she saw me. My entire body felt warm. I'd never loved anything as much as I did Whisper. Just knowing something that special was *mine* made me feel incredibly lucky.

"Oooh, Lauren! She's so beautiful."

"Thanks." I grinned. "We haven't been partners for long, so we've got a lot of work to do. But I love her."

I stroked the mare's cheek while Khloe scratched under her forelock.

"How did you find her?" Khloe asked.

Khloe had spoken the magic words. There was nothing I loved to talk about more than Whisper.

"My old riding instructor, Kim, knew someone who had a good reputation for buying and selling horses. I tried a *lot* of horses before Whisper. None of them were right for me. I was so worried! I didn't even know if I'd find the right one in time for school."

"That had to be a ton of pressure on top of starting Canterwood," Khloe said. She was a great listener. She listened just as enthusiastically as she spoke.

I nodded in agreement. "I was really down about it— worrying about finding a horse, questioning my decision to even come to Canterwood, even whether I was doing the right thing by leaving my boyfriend."

Khloe held up a hand. "Stop. Right. There."

"What?" I said, laughing.

"You said *boyfriend*. I know you just met me, but you don't mention a 'boyfriend' to a girl and expect not to have a bigger conversation about that. You're so not getting away with dropping that detail. We're *so* having that convo later!"

I giggled—I loved Khloe's honesty. "Deal," I said. "But you have to spill in return."

"Well, what are we waiting for?" Khloe asked, grinning. "Let's go to The Sweet Shoppe—a place you will get to know *very* well—grab dessert, then go back to our room. We can talk boys, compare class schedules, and maybe do some unpacking and decorating?"

"Sounds perfect."

I gave Whisper a final pat and we started down the aisle.

Khloe waved to a bunch of people on our way out. She seemed like the *It Girl* of the stable. But not in a way where everyone was afraid of her or sucking up because they felt like they *had* to. The people who flashed smiles at us seemed to genuinely like Khloe.

A feeling of giddiness and relief swept over me. I couldn't have gotten luckier with my roommate.

We walked across the clipped lawn and up the sidewalk toward The Sweet Shoppe.

"Just a sec," I said, stopping to pull out my BlackBerry. "Photo op," I explained to Khloe.

I snapped a pic of the Shoppe and sent it to Chatter, writing, *So adorable! I think this will be my fave hangout spot.* ☺, as the picture's caption.

"This place is the best," Khloe said. "They have killer desserts and they change with the seasons. Right now, it's slushies and ice cream."

"Point me toward the slushies!"

The Sweet Shoppe was cute and old-fashioned-looking with a blue and white awning. A sign hung above that read THE SWEET SHOPPE in scripty font. Khloe pulled open the door for me.

"After you, dah-lin'," she said.

"Why thank you, mademoiselle," I said, smiling. Khloe kept surprising me with her theatricality. I loved the way she laughed at herself and never took herself too seriously.

It made it easy to like her.

Inside the shop, there were blue and white booths, white tables with blue chairs and, in front of us, a glass counter filled with rows upon rows of cookies, with slices of cake and pie underneath. Behind the barista was a soft-serve ice cream machine and containers of sprinkles. A half-dozen slushie machines swirled different colors—pink, red, blue, green.

I peered at a chalkboard menu to see if I was actually reading it right.

"If that really says 'watermelon,' you might never get me out of here," I said.

Khloe laughed. "It does. Wait till you try their peach mango! If you ask for a flavor guide, the baristas give you one that shows how different combos can be made by

mixing flavors. I got pineapple-strawberry once and it was ahh-maze."

"Ooh, *yum*."

Ahead of us, a guy in boots and breeches waited off to the side for his order. His short, shiny black hair contrasted with his blue eyes—a deeper blue than my own. His skin was pale and flawless and a charming smile came easily to his face when he accepted a blue slushie from the barista.

Our eyes connected for a moment before he passed Khloe and me, as he headed for the door.

Chills.

Not that I was exactly ready to start *looking* at guys. Even though this one *was* cute. Very cute. Still, it was too soon after my ex-boyfriend, Taylor, and I had mutually agreed to break up when I left for Canterwood.

Khloe turned, looking back behind us, then stared at me openmouthed.

"Lauren!"

"What?" I said innocently, though I could feel my cheeks burning.

Khloe eyed me warily. "You are *so* crushing on Drew! Look at how red you are!"

I shook my head as we stepped up to the counter.

"Who's Drew? And no, I'm not crushing on *anyone*— named Drew or otherwise. Remember? I told you I left a boy to come here."

"Yeeeaaah." Khloe's eyebrows went up. "That conversation is starting the second we get to our room."

She looked so serious that I almost laughed.

7

SPILLING SECRETS

"START TALKING," KHLOE SAID THE MOMENT our door closed.

I giggled. "Okay, okay."

We kicked off our shoes and Khloe sat in the middle of her bed, her back resting against the wall. I got on my bed—eyeing my box labeled *bedding*—and stretched onto my stomach.

"At home, I dated a really sweet, amazing guy for about five months," I said.

Khloe leaned forward, taking a giant sip of slushie. "Name?"

"Taylor," I said.

She squinted her eyes. "That's a good name. What does he look like?"

"Short blond hair, gorgeous green eyes, tan. Some freckles on his face. He's a swimmer."

"Cute!" Khloe said. "Love jocks." She looked at the ceiling. "And freckles . . . ah-dorable. Continue."

"He and I were both athletes," I said. "So he understood why I needed to practice riding so much. He *always* asked about my lessons and we talked about his swim meets, too."

Khloe gave me a soft smile. "He sounds amazing."

Just thinking about Tay made my chest hurt a little. I could almost smell the chlorine-slash-peppermint mix of his hair as if he was sitting in the room with us.

"He's *totally* amazing," I agreed. "When I found out about my acceptance, we sort of . . . froze. Neither of us wanted to break up, but we wanted the best for each other. As much as neither of us wanted to admit it, 'the best' wasn't staying together, hardly seeing one another."

Khloe made a sad puppy face and I cleared my throat and sat up a little straighter. What was my problem? I'd been fine about the way Tay and I had left things. Hadn't I?

"Long-distance relationships," Khloe concluded, "never work out. You did the right thing."

"He deserved to have a chance to date someone he could actually go *out* with. And he wanted the same for me."

Khloe sipped her slushie. "Wow. Not many guys would be that mature. It sounds like he really, really cared about you. It's probably hard being away from him?"

"Yeah," I said, nodding. "But breaking up was the right thing to do. One hundred percent. Which doesn't mean I can even *think* about him being with another girl yet. We decided to stay friends and had a fun summer hanging out. I can't not have him in my life."

"OMG, it's *just* like *Pretty in Port Royal*," Khloe gasped, clasping her hands. "Lovers forced to be away from one another because of distance. A boy and a girl secretly wanting each other, but agreeing to be friends instead."

I shook my head, biting back my smile and taking a deliberately loud sip of my drink.

Khloe flopped on her back, her hand across her forehead. "Taylor will be away at Yates thinking about his quote—*friend*—unquote ex-girlfriend at Canterwood. Then, he'll see you over Skype and he'll want you back. Old flames will ignite—"

"'Old flames,'" I repeated. "You really *should* audition for a soap. Like, right now. That was exactly like a script of a two o'clock drama."

"Seriously!" she insisted. "He'll want you. You'll want him. But wait . . . a Canterwood guy will be sure to start

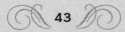

43

paying some attention. Probably more than one—but there will be one you like back," Khloe continued. "Then you'll be *torn* between a long-distance relationship or a . . . Hot. New. Fling."

"Whoa, whoa, whoa!" I laughed. "No relationships. No hot new flings. Break," I said, saying the last word slowly. "I haven't been single long enough to even *think* about other guys. And no way are Tay and I getting back together. I'm happy. He's happy. The end."

"For now." Khloe giggled.

"I think it's time the tables get turned."

Khloe sat up straighter and tucked stray blond locks behind her ears. "Ask me anything."

"Okay, what about you? Any boyfriends past or present?" I asked.

Khloe kicked her slushie with one last, long sip. "Over the summer, I met a guy through our mutual friend in Boston. Neither of us let it get too serious, though, because we both knew I'd be going back to Canterwood in the fall and that he'd leave for his own boarding school in North Carolina."

"What about Canterwood guys?" I asked. "No big crush on anyone or an ex I should know not to like, out of solidarity?"

"Hmm . . ." Khloe rested her head in her hand. "I used

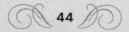

to like this one guy in my theater class, but he didn't feel it. He just looked at me as a theater partner."

"What makes you so sure?" I asked. "It *was* a theater class after all. Maybe he was covering his crushing by acting like you were just a friend."

"No way. We ran lines, we had scenes together—if he liked me, I'd have known. Plus, he had plenty of chances to ask me out."

"Does he know you're interested?"

"Well, I've been kind of subtle . . ."

"*You?*" I asked teasingly. "Khloe Kinsella, we may have just met—but already, I can say with certainty that there is not a subtle bone in your body."

Khloe laughed until tears ran down her face and I raised my now-empty slushie cup to her. "A toast to the fact that we live in the now," I said. "It's not 1940, which means we don't have to wait for guys to ask us out. We are totally in control of our own destinies."

Khloe hopped off her bed and knocked her cup against mine. "Exactly. This year, we control our own fate. It's like our secret roomie pinky-swear. Deal?"

"Deal!"

Khloe knelt down in front her zebra-print suitcase. "And now that the roommate bonding has been sealed

with a slushie, the not-so-pleasant task of unpacking shall commence."

When she unzipped her suitcase, it burst open like a clothes volcano. I couldn't believe how many things she'd gotten to fit! She must have had to sit on top of it to get it zipped shut.

As I opened each carefully wrapped and labeled uber-organized box on my side of the room, Khloe opened a couple of her own boxes. After a flurry of ripped tape and tangled box flaps whirled on Khloe's side of the room, she finally emerged from a tallish box on top of her bed with a handful of purple hangers.

"I learned my lesson last year," she said. "It's best to try and unpack everything before classes start. Decorating, too. Once we're thrown into school tomorrow, we'll have almost zero free time."

"On it," I said.

I had to admit, no matter how chaotic Khloe's packing and unpacking might have seemed, there was a definite method to her madness. This clearly wasn't her first time moving around either. Because no matter how well I'd organized every item of mine that I'd packed, or how methodically I *unpacked*, Khloe and I appeared to be going at the same pace.

Mostly, we worked in a comfortable silence, only stopping to admire each other's stuff or ask each other the occasional question.

I worked my way through box after box—finally getting to the pièce de résistance—the oversized box marked *bedding*. I slid the scissors under the tape and carefully cut an opening along the top of the box. I pulled out my pale blue sheets, matching pillowcases and, finally, inside a thick plastic bag, my brand-new comforter. It was my favorite color: a tropical shade of blue with a gorgeous pink and white argyle print. It was the most gorgeous comforter I'd ever seen and I was so excited to use it!

I arranged alternating cotton candy shades of blue and pink throw pillows on top of my comforter that matched perfectly. Then, I folded up a white plush blanket and laid it at the foot of the bed. The cozy blanket was a fave of mine—perfect to read or study under.

I stepped back and looked at my new bed. I was proud of the bed I'd picked out. The look was preppy, but the colors and texture of the throw pillows gave it a girly-but-not-too-girly feel. Just like me. I'd put together a bed that was the perfect reflection of me—athletic and not afraid to speak out, but also a girly-girl who loved fashion magazines and style icons like Audrey Hepburn and Jackie O.

"Wow!"

I had been so deep in concentration that when Khloe squeaked, it literally made me jump. I searched Khloe's expression, trying to figure out what she was thinking. She was staring at a spot just past me.

"Lauren," she said. "I *love* your bed! It's so . . . you. I can just tell."

I smiled, proud of my work and looked at Khloe's bed—an explosion of furry zebra-print pillows and every shade of purple imaginable.

"You too!" I told her, meaning it.

Khloe put her hands on her hips. "We are going to have the best-decorated room in all of Canterwood's campus."

I liked the way she thought—and I genuinely did love Khloe's side of the room—it was gorgeous, soft, and just crazy enough to be totally chic.

"You know what?" I said. "I think you're right."

Khloe put an arm around my shoulders. "I think we're going to *shop* very well together."

"So true," I said, thinking about the Pottery Barn Teen credit card my parents had given me over the summer. The card was "exclusively for shopping for my dorm

room"—*and* my emergency Visa card had come with a stern warning that if I got to school and didn't get good grades, I'd lose both, as well as any future allowance for a *long* time.

"How hard *are* classes here?" I asked. The thought of disappointing my parents—and, okay, losing my spending privileges—made me anxious. "I came from what *I* thought of as a pretty tough prep school, but Canterwood's summer homework alone was almost like a full-time job."

"If you made it through the summer work, you'll be fine," Khloe said. She picked up a cheery yellow shower caddy. It was filled with shampoo, conditioner, hair styling products, face wash, shower gel, a razor and shaving cream. I noticed that we were both Bumble and bumble girls—down to the same coconut-scented shampoo.

"You're sure?" I asked when she came back from the bathroom.

"Totally," she said. "Look—classes *are* tough. But you were *chosen* to come here. Summer work is kind of like a big test." She paused. "I know these twins who were admitted last year and they couldn't finish their summer homework."

My eyes widened. "So what happened?"

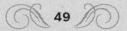

Khloe played with the cap on her Bumble and bumble Surf spray. "Headmistress Drake had to call their parents," she said softly, setting the spray on top of her dresser.

I cringed.

"Drake told them that anyone who could not complete the summer work would certainly not be able to keep up with the pace at Canterwood. She told them to leave and the two girls went back to their old school immediately."

"No way! How did you even hear about this?"

Khloe shifted her weight to the other foot. "Actually? They're my sisters."

8

KISMET

THE LOOK ON MY FACE MUST HAVE DONE A good job conveying how mortified I was to have brought up such a bad topic.

"Lauren, it's okay. *You* didn't kick them out!"

"I just feel bad I even brought it up. Did your family want you to leave?"

"No way," Khloe said. "It was totally the twins' fault. They were so excited about Canterwood because they wanted to go away and live on their own, but they didn't take work seriously." She shook her head. "I hope I didn't scare you. I meant to reassure you that summer work really prepped you for this year. Canterwood moves at a crazy pace. Stay with it and stick it out. Just don't fall behind."

"Thanks," I said. "For the advice, I mean. It's a little daunting—and a lot to take in."

"Anytime—and don't worry so much. You'll get used to it." Khloe smiled and went back to our bathroom, shower curtain in hand. It was a pretty light yellow with white daisies. We'd agreed on it via e-mail.

I glanced over at her closet. It looked liked a rainbow now that she'd finished. She definitely had a bold, happy style. I liked that.

I unpacked my lamp—a *très* chic PBteen purchase. It had a clear acrylic base and blue lampshade that matched my bedspread. Tiny crystals dangled all around the bottom of the shade. I added a framed photo of Becca, Charlotte, Mom, Dad, and me to my nightstand. In the picture, we were all seated outdoors at a French bistro. It had been taken this summer on a trip to New York City.

I turned to a small, heavy box labeled *books*. I opened it up and started stacking a few books at a time on the second shelf of my nightstand.

The second I touched the cover, I knew I had *it*. The book that made my room feel like home. My tea guide book. Under it, I found my tea journal. They fit nicely together on my white nightstand.

Tea was my addiction. Back when we'd lived in

Brooklyn, our brownstone had gotten so cold in the winter that Mom made tea to keep me and my sisters warm. She used a tea kettle to heat the water, so I knew whenever I heard the whistle that I'd soon be holding a warm mug of something delicious between my palms.

As I'd gotten older, I started to collect tea—loose and bagged—and supplies like a tea strainer and my guide book. I'd always spent some of my allowance money on trying different kinds of tea.

Khloe walked over to my nightstand. "It's starting to look like a real room in here!" she said. "I'm so excited. Can I look at your photo and books?"

"Of course."

I pointed out the people in the photo to Khloe. "That's my stepdad, Gregg, my older sister Charlotte, my other older sister, Becca, and my mom."

"Your eyes are the same color as your stepdad's. That's so cool."

"Isn't it?" I said. "He's been my dad since I was two. My biological dad left when I was a baby. My stepdad's the best."

"What about your sisters?" Khloe asked.

"Becca and I are best friends. Charlotte and I don't get along very well. She's in college at Sarah Lawrence right now. But growing up, we were always competitive with each other. The second I started winning blue ribbons for riding, Charlotte became the star of our school's Scholastic Bowl. I got straight As, so Charlotte got all A-pluses and tutored on the weekends. It's just this ongoing rivalry thing between us that's never gone away."

Khloe frowned. "That's awful. I mean, I'm not *best* friends with Hailey and Michelle—the twins," she reminded me. "But we're pretty close. They've always had the twin thing, though. Like . . . they know what the other is thinking and they do everything together and dress alike."

Khloe got on her knees, touching the spines of my books. She pulled out one I'd read a zillion times—*Fake Me a Match*. I wondered if I'd even have time to read for fun here. "What about your other sister? Does she get along with Charlotte?"

"Becca is the buffer between us. I know that's unfair to her."

Khloe pulled *Everything You Need to Know About Tea and More* from my nightstand. "So," she said. "I guess you're not a fan of tea?"

"Nope." I laughed. "Hate it. And the tea kettle I brought? Just for decoration."

"I drink tea sometimes, too," Khloe said. "I'm usually a coffee girl, but I've heard certain teas are good for your voice?"

"Yeah," I said immediately. "Green tea with honey and lemon would be perfect for you before your audition. It has caffeine and would definitely soothe your throat. I'll make you some—just remind me before the big day."

"I'd love that." Khloe smiled. "Thanks."

I reached for my tea journal—a gift from my aunt. I ran my fingertips over the gorgeous cover—raised ice-blue and silver swirls. Everyone in my family knew my favorite color and always tried to find presents for me in the same shade of blue. I flipped it open to a random page.

"This," I said, holding it out to Khloe. "is my tea journal." She took it, peering at the page. "I write down every tea I've tried, ones I want to try, and if I like a tea or not. I rate them with stars."

"Oooh." Khloe pointed to Celestial Seasonings' white tea with pear. It had ★★★★★ beside it—the highest rating—five out of five. "You must really like that one."

"It's *so* good."

Khloe flipped through the pages. "You'll have to be my tea tutor. There are so many kinds! Like this one . . ." She pointed to a tea three-fourths of the way through the journal. "I've never heard of *red* tea. Green, yes. But *red*? Is it actually red?"

"It is—and there are a ton. Oh, Khloe—you never should have asked me to teach you," I said, shaking my head. "I'll never stop talking. You'll run to the dorm monitor's office and beg for a new roommate."

Khloe giggled. "Christina," she acted out. "My roomie—she is obsessed with tea! It's *terrifying*. I *fear* for my *life*!"

I giggled with her and Khloe looked at me mock-dramatically. "I think I'll keep you anyway." Khloe put back my journal and flashed me an Oscar-worthy smile. "Seriously, Lauren—I am *so* happy we got paired together. Total kismet!"

I smiled. But, "Kismet?" I asked.

"Meant to be!" she sang, skipping over to her bed.

"Oh," I said, nodding in fierce agreement. "Then, 'kismet' it is."

I unpacked the books I'd brought, taking two of the four built-in bookshelves in our room. Next: my desk. The beautiful white-painted wood desk had a center drawer, two curved drawers on each side, and a hutch on top.

Soon my purple HP laptop, flexible desk light, bright

silver wire pen holder and matching paper holders were set up. I filled one drawer with notebooks and another with an organizer that held a stapler, paper clips, erasers, Wite-Out, and other random supplies. When I'd bought everything at Staples this summer, Becca, teasingly, had kept three feet away from me at all times, pretending not to know me as I excitedly filled an entire cart with school supplies.

"You *do* know that you can buy stuff online when you get to school, right?" Becca had asked.

"But then, something important might not get there in time. I mean, what if my order of highlighters doesn't get to school by Monday? Then I have *no highlighters.* I won't be able to take good notes. I'll fail all of my classes on the first day and—"

"Okay, okay!" Becca held up her hands in a conceding gesture. "Continue to fill the cart, Canterwood girl."

The memory made me smile and I tried to ignore the tug of sadness when I thought how far apart Becca and I were now as I finished with my desk. Once I'd finished, I looked at my side of the room. I was especially pleased with my closet where all of my clothes were color coordinated. Khloe hadn't teased me once about my type A organization.

HOME-TYPE
THINGS

BY MIDAFTERNOON, KHLOE AND I WERE BOTH exhausted.

We had put in a DVD from season one of the TV show *Sing*. (We'd screamed and jumped up and down when we found out we were both *Sing* fangirls!) I had all four seasons on DVD, Khloe had a brand-new flat-screen and a Blu-Ray player—*voilà!*

"Kismet, once again!" Khloe had said.

Now we were each in our beds, half watching the show and half—in my case—reeling from information and sensory overload. My eyes were just starting to go from blink to closed-for-nap when my phone buzzed. The BlackBerry Messenger sign was red.

Ana: I saw ur update on Chatter. The Sweet Shoppe looks so cool!

I sat up, already so happy to hear from *someone* at home it almost made me teary.

Lauren: I'm glad you saw it! And, um, HI!!! How are you? How's everything?

Immediately, the screen lit up. *Ana is writing a message . . .*

I waited impatiently for her response.

Ana: LOL. Hi, LT!! Nothing has changed since you left—trust me. Except it's Sat nite & school starts on Mon. ☹ Brielle and I r gonna miss u!

Lauren: It'll b SO weird. Can't imagine classes w/o u guys.

Ana: How IS it? Ur roomie? Ur room? BBM us pix.

Lauren: OK,OK! Will take TONS of pix. ☺ It's amazing. Whisper loves it, 2, I think. My roomie, Khloe, is so cool. Her horse's name is Ever. Bay mare w a ★. Sooo cute!

Ana: That's great, Laur! I'm rlly glad u like Khloe. It would b awful if u guys hated each other.

Lauren: Def. R u ready for school?

Ana: OMG, thanks 2 Brielle (I think), I am TOO ready. She came over & even picked out my 1st day clothes.

Ana: I sketched Bri in action and it came out a giant blur.

Lauren: LOL.

Lauren: That's my 'AnaArtiste.'

I referenced her Chatter handle.

Ana: Has she BBMed u yet? Tay?

Lauren: Not yet. Prob scrambling 4 school.

Ana: I'm sure they'll b in touch soon. We'll all b thinking about u & missing u!

Lauren: Same.

Khloe looked over at my frantic typing. "Old friends?" she asked with a smile.

"Yeah," I said. I returned her smile, but her use of the word "old" made me feel uneasy.

Lauren: Gotta run, but miss u and ttys!

Ana: Mwah! Ttyvs!

Lauren: VVS! ☺

I locked my phone, shoving it back in my pocket.

I hadn't said anything to Ana, but I felt a little down that I *hadn't* heard from Brielle or Taylor. I *could* message them, but I was the one who'd left and I didn't want to seem like a baby, like I was already homesick. Even though . . . *technically* . . . I might have been feeling a tiny bit sick. For . . . home-type things. I took a deep breath. They'd write soon.

They were just as busy as I was. Brielle was probably at the mall—her arms filled with piles of clothes—and Taylor was probably . . . no, definitely . . . in his pool, swimming laps. They weren't going to disappear just because I'd switched schools.

"Hey," Khloe said, catching me off guard. "Want to go make some tea?"

Homey relief rushed through me. *A cup of honey vanilla chamomile tea is exactly what I need,* I thought. The ingredients always calmed me down.

"That," I said. "Is the best idea ever."

I was beginning to realize—new friends could sometimes make you feel just as good as old ones could.

10

TEA? PARTY!

THE COMMON ROOM IN HAWTHORNE LOOKED like something out of Charlotte's Sarah Lawrence catalog.

A bunch of students were inside, two on a sectional sofa-slash-chaise watching the flat-screen mounted on the pastel purple–painted wall. Others, curled up in recliners, read or texted. The room, which I'd expected to feel institutional, felt warm and inviting.

There were shelves of books and DVDs, a couple of gaming systems and a full kitchen. While I warmed the kettle on the stove, Khloe sat on the counter, talking to one of the girls I'd met this morning. No matter how hard I tried, I couldn't remember her name!

Once I'd finished making the tea, I made my way to Khloe and . . . and . . . ugh! I was going to seem *so* rude if I made it obvious I didn't know her name. I tried, telepathically, to make Khloe say her name the second I got over to them.

"This looks fun!" Khloe said, taking tea boxes from my hand. "Like we should have a tea party or something."

What was her name?!

The girl brushed a stray curl out of her face and smiled at me. "I know we met in the frenzy of this morning. But you've probably met a million people today. My name is Lexa Reed. Friend of drama-queen Khloe Kinsella."

I breathed a huge sigh of relief.

"Lexa, of course! I'm Lauren Towers. New roommate of drama-queen Khloe Kinsella."

"Towers—aha! That's why Khlo's been calling you 'LT,'" said Lexa.

I raised an eyebrow at Khloe.

"That's right," Khloe said, pointing at me. "You have been nicknamed. I declared it so."

I looked at Lexa. "I guess I've been nicknamed." I laughed, not having the heart to tell her people called me "LT" all the time.

Lexa laughed, too. She had an awesome laugh, one of those super infectious laughs, even when no one knows why she's laughing.

"I think," Lexa said. "that you've been Khloe'd in general."

"Is that a good thing, being 'Khloe'd'?" Khloe asked amid all of our laughter. "Or a bad thing?"

"Definitely good," Lexa said. She squeezed Khloe's hand with hers. "We all need a little Khloe in our lives."

"Agreed," I said, raising my hand to vote.

Khloe grinned. She looked very proud of herself. "Oooh! Is the tea ready?" she asked.

I nodded, handing her a mug.

"Want any?" I offered Lexa.

"Thanks! I'd love some," Lexa said, accepting the mug. "My roommate, Jill, is still unpacking. I could use a break."

"We really should have a tea party!" Khloe said. She held out her mug, extra daintily. "I've never practiced sipping tea like a lady. Who knows? It might come up in an audition."

Lexa's eyes met mine. She gave me a *she really is like this all the time* look.

"A tea party sounds fabulous," I said.

"Feel free to choose a tea," I said, offering Lexa a box filled with an array of my favorite white teas, plus, a couple of black ones.

"Khloe, I made you honey vanilla chamomile and sweetened it with clove honey, like mine. Next time, I'll make you Earl Grey and serve it with Hobnobs so you can practice for your lead in a period drama."

Lexa's eyes widened. "Hobnobs? You really know your stuff!"

"Seriously?" I asked. "You know what Hobnobs are?"

I'd never met anyone else who knew about the yummy chocolate-coated cookies that were popular in the UK.

"I lived in London for a long time with my family— Hobnobs were my fave!"

Khloe looked at the two of us as though we were aliens. "Why are you guys speaking a weird language?" she asked, taking a tentative sip of her tea. "Oooh! Yum!"

"You look shocked," I said, holding my hand to my chest in mock offense. "And Hobnobs are these amazing cookies—"

"Covered in chocolate!" Lexa cut in.

"Exactly." I nodded. "British people serve them with tea."

"Sounds delish," Khloe said, sipping her tea again. "And for the record, I'm *impressed*, not shocked."

Lexa turned to me. "So, I used to live in London, but how did you find out about Hobnobs?"

"Weird language," Khloe repeated. "But to answer

your question, LT knows about the weird cookies because she knows absolutely everything and *anything* about all things tea."

I felt my cheeks warm and buried my face in my tea. "Well," I said between sips, "not *everything*. I mean—"

"She's cute because she's humble," Khloe teased.

I rolled my eyes at myself and offered the box of tea to Lexa again. Lexa picked up a packet of spearmint tea. "This sounds refreshing. It's so hot outside."

"That really will cool you down," I said. "And it's good with ice, too. But I only brought two mugs."

Khloe opened a cabinet above the microwave and motioned to the shelves as though she were modeling on a game show.

The cabinet was filled top to bottom with mugs. Dragonflies, horses, funny sayings. Green mugs adorned with yellow-gold Canterwood logos.

Lexa took a GO CANTERWOOD! mug and opened a drawer next to the stove. It was filled with sugar packets, Sweet'N Low, Sugar In The Raw, and my fave—Splenda. Lexa plucked out two banana-yellow packets of Splenda and shut the drawer with her hip. I unwrapped her bag of spearmint tea and placed it in her mug. She ripped open the two Splendas and poured the contents in. I made

sure no one's fingers were anywhere but the mug handle before pouring the steaming kettle water in last.

"Thanks, Lauren!" Lexa said.

"Now it's an official tea party!" Khloe said. "Let's grab the window seat and chat."

Lexa and I followed Khloe. The window seat was tucked away from the center of the common room.

We sank into the black cushions, Khloe and I with our backs against the wall and Lexa cross-legged in the middle. The window looked out over the tennis court and outdoor pool. Two of Canterwood's many facilities that I couldn't wait to use.

"So, when did *you* start at Canterwood?" I asked Lexa, gesturing to her with my mug.

"Sixth grade," she said. "Same year as Khlo. My parents sent me here for the academics, but I came to *ride*."

"Oh, yay! Another rider!" I grinned. "Did you bring your own horse?"

"Only the love of my life! My mare, Honor," Lexa said. "You?"

"I've got a mare, too. Her name's Whisper and I just got her over the summer, so we're still getting used to each other. But I totally understand what you mean. I'm already so in love with Whisper. I can't imagine how I'll feel after we've had a whole year to bond."

"Whisper's *such* a pretty name," Lexa said. "I bet our horses are all going to be friends."

Khloe looked back and forth between us, smiling like she was keeping the juiciest secret ever kept!

"KK, you know you want to spill something," Lexa said, beating me to it.

"Yeah," I encouraged. "I don't know all of your tell-tale 'looks' yet . . . but even *I* can tell you're dying to say something. So I agree with Lexa—spill away." I smiled to encourage her further.

"It's just . . . tea party love. My new *roomie* and my best *bestie* are bonding." She fanned her eyes with her right hand, fingers splayed, pretending to fight off tears. "It's a lovefest."

Lexa rolled her eyes but we were both laughing. "Aaand . . . we can bond *even more* if we have classes together," Lexa teased. She half stood, pulling a folded piece of paper from the back pocket of her jeans. "Schedules?"

"Mine's in our room," Khloe said.

"Mine too," I said.

Khloe set her mug on the table next to her. "I glanced at it, but I don't remember it at all. I'll grab it. Lauren, want me to get yours?"

"Mine's on top of my desk," I said. "Thank you so much, Khlo."

Khloe held up her hands in a stop-everything motion. "Did you just say *Khlo*?" she asked.

Oh *no*. My first day and I'd already called my roommate by a name she clearly *hated*.

"Omigod, I'm so—"

"I've been LT'd!" Khloe broke in joyously.

"Wait," I said, heart pounding. "You *liked* when I called you that?"

Lexa broke in as Khloe nodded emphatically. "Way to traumatize your new roommate on day one." Lexa shook her head.

"How?" Khloe asked. "I got LT'd—she gave me a nickname. That's how we do!"

"Because I like you," Lexa said to me with a smile. "I'm going to give you a crash course in Khloe 101."

"I'll take it!" I said. I made a come-here motion with my hands. "Lay it on me."

"First: never take her too seriously."

"Got it," I said.

"Except—and this is rule number two—if you see tears."

"Really?"

"Really," Lexa said. "Khloe *never* cries. So if she does, something is *wrong*. And last?"

"Yes?"

"Khloe is the funnest person of anyone I know. You won the roommate lottery." Lexa smiled kindly. "And from what I can tell, so did she. So *have fun*. This school can get so *serious*. You and KK seem good for each other. Just don't steal her away completely."

Despite the smile on her face, I detected a hint of seriousness in that one and I took note that Lexa liked people in her circle to share. She was the cutest—and had been nothing but kind to me. But still, I wouldn't want to get on her bad side.

"I'd never steal her," I promised. "Not that she'd stand for being stolen."

Lexa laughed. "Sounds like you've got it down. Nah, you don't need my help."

"Like I said—I take everything I can get," I said again.

"The way Canterwood lets us set up our schedules is so cool," I said to Lexa, changing the subject. "At my old school, we had to meet with a guidance counselor who pretty much decided our schedules *for* us based on previous classes and test scores. This way is so much better."

"It's actually new for seventh graders and above," Lexa said. "Last year, we had to meet with a guidance counselor too—Ms. Utz, you'll meet her soon enough. She basically helped us decide our schedules. The new system is *so* much easier."

"I *might* have obsessed about it a teensy bit," I said, totally understating the degree of my obsession.

"Obsessed to the point where I'd needed an intervention" would've been more accurate. I'd spent hours every day of summer break looking at the Canterwood course catalog. I'd received a copy of the eighty-three page catalog. *Eighty-three* pages! For seventh graders alone! I read the catalog cover to cover multiple times. I highlighted. I sticky-noted.

At one point, Becca, half-asleep, had stumbled into my room at three in the morning one of the many nights when I'd been up with a sticky tab on every finger and a highlighter permanently affixed to my right hand. Without saying a word, she'd taken the catalog from me and walked out of my room. The next morning, I crawled into bed with her and she pulled the catalog out from under her pillow. She told me she'd done it for my own good and that if I didn't choose my classes *today*, she'd do it herself and mail it in.

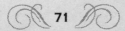

Khloe held my schedule out for me to take it and snapped me back to reality. She pulled up a chair, facing Lexa and me.

The schedule swap was on!

II

SCHEDULE SWAP

"LET'S SEE WHAT WE'VE GOT," KHLOE SAID, tracing her schedule with her right pointer finger. "We *better* have some classes together or this will be the worst year of my entire life!" She sat back in her chair, fanning herself with the paper.

Lexa, smiling, rolled her eyes, and looked at me, holding up one finger—as in, rule number one—don't take anything Khloe says too seriously.

I made a check mark motion in the air so she knew I got it.

She turned to Khloe. "I'd give that performance a B minus," she told her.

Khloe's mouth fell open. "No way. B *plus*, easy."

Lexa shook her head. "The best I can do is a solid B."

Khloe paused, contemplating this. "Was it the fanning? I knew I was pushing it."

Lexa shrugged. "The fanning is too dramatic."

"Hmm. Okay, I can take direction," Khloe said. "No fan."

"You could have made wide eyes and chewed your bottom lip," I suggested, playing along with the banter.

Khloe put a hand over her heart. "When I'm accepting my first Oscar, I'll thank you both in my speech."

"What about your second Oscar?" Lexa asked.

Khloe shook her head, a serious expression on her face. "Oh, no—I'll be waaay too famous and important by then. I'll have forgotten you long ago."

We laughed together and I finally looked at my paper.

"Okay, I've got math with Ms. Utz," I said.

"Me too!" Khloe and Lexa said at the same time.

We high-fived.

"American history with Mr. Spellman," I said.

Khloe smiled. "Same."

"Count me out," Lexa said.

"English with Mr. Davidson," I continued.

"You're stuck with me again," Khloe said.

"Not it," Lexa said.

"French III with Madame LaFleur," I offered.

Khloe and Lexa shook their heads. "Spanish I with Señora Garcia," Lexa said.

"I've got her, too," Khloe said.

The two friends smiled at each other.

"I can't believe you're taking French *III*," Lexa said. "That's waaay advanced. Most *ninth* graders don't even take it."

"I took French at my old school," I said. "And I studied it on my own. I love the way it sounds—it's such a romantic language."

I looked back at my schedule. "Gym twice a week with Mr. Warren."

"Gym?" Khloe asked. "Why are you taking that?"

"It's not required for students who participate in a sport," Lexa explained.

"I know . . . ," I said, hesitating to explain. "I wanted to stay extra strong for riding."

"You're insane," Khloe said. "After you've climbed the rope for the fiftieth time, you'll be wondering why you didn't drop it."

"Maybe," I said. "But my next class—life science?— sounds interesting. With Ms. Meade?"

"We're in the same class," Lexa said. "But I'm not as interested as you seem."

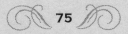

I stared at my schedule again. "All I have left is study hall twice a week and my elective—fashion," I said. "I'd take that class every day if it was offered!"

"Ah, so we have a fashionista among us," Lexa said, seeming intrigued.

"I had a feeling you were into fashion. I bet you like classical American fashion, maybe? That's the impression I got from your clothes," Khloe said.

I stared at her. "That's only the highest compliment ever. Jackie O. and Audrey Hepburn are my style icons. I'm really into reinventing old looks so that they seem fresh."

When I'd read that Canterwood offered fashion as an elective, I'd practically screamed. I BlackBerry messaged all of my friends with a dozen *!!!!!!*s and immediately starred it as a definite course. After I enrolled, I posted an update on Chatter.

LaurBell: Ahhh! I'm taking *fashion* at Canterwood this fall! So excited! I remembered Ana's reply, smiling.

AnaArtiste: @LaurBell Hmm . . . all this time as your BFF and I had no clue you liked fashion. ;P

"Without question, I know Khloe's elective is acting," I said.

Khloe grinned from ear to ear.

"What's yours?" I asked Lexa.

"Website design," Lexa said. "I'm really big into online artistry. I already promised KK that as soon as I was ready, I'd create her own personal website complete with acting portfolio."

"I'm excited," I said. "But it definitely sounds like we're all going to be busy."

"Definitely." Khloe folded her schedule. "Oh—plus glee club."

"As if," I said. "Not that I'll even make it. I'm just excited to audition."

"I've watched the glee club perform before games and school events," Lexa said. "Everyone always looks like they're having so much fun—and they do super contemporary stuff, which is cool." She peered at my schedule again. "Now that I'm looking at it on paper, your schedule is *really* full. A ton of advanced classes, plus riding *and* glee club."

I scanned my paper. "*Maybe* glee club. But I don't seem to have more than you or Khloe. Plus, riding and glee and fashion are all things I *live* for." My smile sunk a little. "You think it's too much?"

"I think Lexa just meant you're taking those AP classes, so it might mean more homework," Khloe said. "It's your first year, is all. We just want you to be careful to ease into things so you don't overextend yourself."

"I won't," I promised. Lexa and Khloe still seemed concerned, but they'd see—I'd just have to *prove* that I could handle the courses.

We spent a few more minutes chatting about classes before it was dinner time. Khloe and Lexa waited in the hallway while I put away my tea and two mugs.

As we walked, I checked my phone—two BBMs.

Taylor: How's it going, Canterwood girl?

Brielle: Laur! How's everything?! I need deets!

I knew *exactly* who I was three-way conference calling when I got back from dinner. Smiling, I followed Khloe and Lexa to the dining hall—to my first official dinner as a student at Canterwood. Looking from my new room-mate to my new friend (I hoped), I wondered how long it had taken *them* to feel like real Canterwood students.

12

WHISPER, WE'RE NOT AT BRIAR CREEK ANYMORE

IN THE SUNDAY MORNING DARKNESS, I SLIPPED out of bed and grabbed the clothes I'd laid out the night before.

It was barely dawn and I was on my way to the stable to visit Whisper.

I loved getting up with the sun. I was definitely a morning person. I tiptoed to the bathroom, dressed in breeches, a lilac and white striped V-neck T-shirt and paddock boots. Being a morning person in a houseful of night owls had taught me the invaluable skill of moving around without making one sound. In the bathroom, I brushed my hair, putting it into a loose, faux-messy bun. I washed my face and applied tinted sunscreen and ran through the rest of my routine, thinking about last night's dinner with Khloe and Lexa.

I saw that Clare—Khloe's other friend—sat alone across the cafeteria until Khloe's arch-nemesis, Riley, walked over to her with a few other girls I didn't know.

Khloe waved at Clare, but the two definitely stayed separated at all times in the cafeteria. It felt as if Riley had drawn an invisible line between Khloe and Clare.

Once I was all ready to go, I left a gently snoring Khloe in our room and walked down Hawthorne's hallway. Even our dorm monitor, Christina, wasn't up yet. Every single dorm room door was closed. Silent. No TV, no laughter, no ringing phones. Not even a whisper was audible.

I pushed open the door and walked down the sidewalk. The fiery sun rose over one of the pastures and horses' backs began to be illuminated in the light. Like a shadow was being lifted from the campus.

I passed the gym, then the pool, and started past the tennis courts. Two older girls, engaged in a fierce tennis match, were red-faced as they darted back and forth across the court—slamming the ball over the net.

The old-fashioned streetlamps made the campus look *très parfait*. Like a framed painting. The lamps turned off as soon as the sunlight hit them.

My pace quickened as I walked down the sidewalk, passing through the courtyard and nearing the stable.

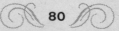

I couldn't wait to see Whisper.

I hoped her first night on campus had been as good as mine.

The stable's sliding white doors were open. So . . . I wasn't the *only* one here early. Several students were around. Some mucked out stalls, cleaned tack, organized tack trunks or even bathed horses in the wash stalls.

This isn't Briar Creek, I reminded myself.

If I'd gone to my old stable this early, I would have been the only student there for several hours. This many riders here before six on a Sunday morning told me one thing: *I have to be on.* There were too many great, dedicated riders here for me to slack even for one second. I would have to be at the stable as much as possible and put everything I had into riding.

Tomorrow was my test ride from which Mr. Conner would place me in the beginner or intermediate team. Over the summer, all the new seventh-grade riders got an e-mail from Mr. Conner, explaining how the testing system worked. Apparently, it had changed from last year.

Incoming seventh graders would test for the beginner or intermediate team. Returning students already on the beginner or intermediate team would test the following week so long as they'd been on the same team for a full school year.

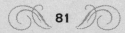

Last year, a couple of talented sixth graders, including Khloe, had tested into the advanced team, where they would start this year. The intermediate pool would be bigger this year—with room for up to six students. I wondered how many of those six slots were actually occupied.

I headed for Whisper's stall near the end of the aisle. I spotted someone familiar next to Whisper's stall—a petite girl with curly dark hair pinned back with glittery purple barrettes. *Oooh, the barrettes!* J'adore!

Lexa took a halter and lead line out of her tack trunk. She looked up when I stopped at Whisper's gleaming wooden tack trunk.

"Hey, neighbor," Lexa said.

"Oh, cool," I said. "This is perfect."

I felt so guilty last night after all the time I'd spent with Khloe and Lex. I hated not being truthful with two incredibly nice people who honestly wanted to be friends. Still, every time I thought about telling the truth about my riding background, my . . . accident, I'd stopped.

No. Canterwood was my fresh start. And if that meant leaving out some details about my career as a competitive rider, who would really even care?

"Come meet Honor," Lexa said.

A strawberry roan with a blaze stuck her head over the door and nudged Lexa's shoulder. Lexa laughed and stroked the horse's muzzle.

"I guess she wants to introduce herself," Lexa said, laughing. "This is Honor. She's just a *little* outgoing."

"A tiny bit," I said, laughing.

I reached my hand up for the mare to smell. Her nostrils widened as she took in my scent, then stuck her head in my direction. "She's beautiful," I said, truthfully.

Lexa leaned against the stall door, rubbing Honor's cheek. "Thank you. I got her a couple of years ago. She'd just turned five."

"What breed?" I asked.

"Saddlebred and Thoroughbred mix. She's got the smooth gait and long strides of a Saddlebred and the speed of a Thoroughbred."

The mare bumped Lexa's shoulder with her cheek. "And the energy of a yearling!" Lexa added.

Whisper, likely hearing my voice, put her head over the stall door. I stepped over to her and Lexa followed me.

"This is my girl, Whisper," I said. The mare reached her cashmere-soft muzzle toward me. I ran my finger over the pink and white snip on her muzzle. Her coat, the lightest shade of gray, almost shimmered.

"I love grays!" Lexa said. "She's tall, too. What breed?"

"It took a while for me to find out," I explained. "My riding instructor helped me purchase her from a reputable breeder, but Whisper was a special case. She was originally bought at auction from people who didn't give the breeder much information about her past. Finally, I learned that Whisper is a double registered Hanoverian and Thoroughbred."

"What a great mix," Lexa said. "I love her delicate face and the contrast with her strong body."

"Strong body *and* strong will," I added.

Strong will was definitely the right description, without a doubt. Whisper was sweet and she listened to every single command I gave her. But there were still a few kinks to work out. Every time I got frustrated, I reminded myself that we were still new to each other. Not to mention that I hadn't been able to spend as much time at the stable as I'd wanted.

Maybe because my to-do list had looked something like this:

- ☐ CARPET FOR END OF BED
- ☐ NIGHTSTAND
- ☐ LAMP/SHADE

☐ iPod dock

☐ desk

☐ storage containers . . .

That part of the to-buy list had gone on and on *and on*. The rest of the list?

☐ Do Canterwood summer homework.

☐ Register for classes.

☐ Buy new clothes.

☐ Pack old clothes.

☐ Pack accessories.

☐ Study Canterwood campus map.

. . . and the list kept going.

When I'd finally found Whisper—my perfect horse match—I thought I'd spend all summer getting to ride. But prepping for school had taken more time than I'd thought.

Lexa shifted, pulling me out of my thoughts. "I wouldn't be too nervous about having a new horse here. No one better than Mr. Conner to train you both."

"I hope so," I said, hoping I wasn't showing the nervousness I felt. "Because I'm testing for the intermediate team tomorrow."

"I'm sure you'll do great! I hope we're on the same team. I tested into intermediate at the end of last year. There are five riders on the team this year, so there's one open seat."

One spot?

"Do you know how many new students are trying out?"

"Well, it won't just be new students," Lexa said. "Seventh graders who were on the beginner team and want to move up will test, too. So, if I had to guess, I'd say . . . fifteen or so?"

"Fifteen?" I could only manage one word. "Wait, what happens to the students who don't make the intermediate team?"

"Canterwood accepts anyone into the riding program," Lexa said. "Some students just pleasure ride and aren't on a team to compete. The school takes any student who wants to try out for the beginner team. And there's not just one. There are two beginner teams for seventh grade, so the classes aren't too big—that's where students who don't make the intermediate team go."

"Mr. Conner teaches *all* of those classes?"

"There are two other instructors who teach sixth grade teams and beginner seventh graders," Lexa said. "They're both nice and good instructors."

I wilted a little. I was sure they *were* nice, but I wanted Mr. Conner. Especially after everything I'd heard about him.

"Hey," Lexa said, stroking Whisper's forehead, seeming to address us both. "Try not to even think about that. The best advice I can think of is this: when you ride, ride as if you're already a rider for the intermediate team. Then, when you're in front of Mr. Conner for the first time, ride like you're trying to keep the spot you *already have.* If you got into Canterwood's riding program, you already made it farther than most."

I smiled. "Thanks."

"Don't mention it," said Lexa. "Hey, have you ridden since you got here?"

I shook my head.

"Want me to show you my favorite trail? It'll be fun! I can tell you what testing will be like and catch you up about the riders who are already on the intermediate team."

"I'd love to go! Just knowing what testing will be like will help my nerves a ton."

That and many, many cups of chamomile tea.

"Great. I've got to groom Honor and tack up, but I'll meet you right outside in, say, half an hour?"

"Perfect."

13

THE TOWERS FAMILY
WORK ETHIC

I SLIPPED INTO WHISPER'S STALL, CLOSING the door and wrapping my arms around her neck. She felt like my piece of home.

"I missed you, pretty girl," I said. "What do you think of Canterwood?"

I let go of her neck so I could look into her big brown eyes. I loved when she blinked. She almost looked like she was flirting, with her curly gray eyelashes. I peered over to look at her pink hay net. Empty. The matching water bucket was half full.

"I think someone's settling in just fine," I said. "I'm going to grab your tack—then I'll get you all groomed and extra shiny."

Whisper nudged my arm with her muzzle, her whiskers

tickling me. I patted her shoulder, then walked to the other end of the hallway to grab her tack. The feeling of being at a new stable—people and horses I'd never met milling around me—was something I was actually very used to. Before my accident, I'd competed almost every other weekend at different shows. My trainer and I had purposely set up my schedule so that I could show as often as humanly possible.

My goal had been to rack up enough points to become the season's overall champion. To get a championship title, I had to compete as often as possible in classes with high difficulty and win at least second place. Most of the time, I needed first. If I showed and didn't do well, I didn't earn enough points and had to show more to make up for lost points.

But my goals had changed since then. Now, I was itching to get back to—and perfect—the basics. I knew it was the only way to compete and *sustain* and elevate my competition level.

Inside the tack room, I slid Whisper's saddle and plum-colored pad over my arm. I had a few saddle pads in different, fun colors for practicing and trail riding. The white ones for showing were stowed away, but I also had red, pink, blue, and yellow.

I unzipped the new saddle I'd done chores all summer to save for—an all-purpose Butet saddle from Beval Saddlery Ltd. So, when I finally unwrapped the saddle and touched the buttery soft leather, I was beyond proud that I'd worked hard for to pay for half of it—all on my own. It felt more like *mine* than anything I'd ever owned. When the saddle had arrived in the mail, I'd stared at the sealed box for a long time—almost afraid to open it. The Butet saddle was *not* inexpensive. My parents had only agreed that I could get it because (a) I was paying for half, and (b) it was *extremely* customizable (parent translation: practical.)

I never took for granted that I was lucky to have parents who could provide for me beyond the things I truly needed. My mom, a successful lawyer, had taught us all how to work hard for what we wanted. Same with my dad—a stay-at-home writer. Writing kept him busy most of the day and sometimes all night when he was on deadline. He led by example; he wasn't going to hand us money for a trip to the mall—we had to earn it. None of my sisters nor I had ever been handed anything.

At Yates Preparatory, my old school in Union, there were too many students whose parents gave them whatever they wanted—*whenever* they wanted it. I hadn't really

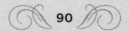

hung out with those kids in school—the rich guys who thought they could buy a girl expensive jewelry and she'd go out with him. And definitely not the wealthy girls who looked at every other girl as if she were speaking an alien language if she admitted to buying her clothes anywhere other than Barneys or Saks.

Ana and Brielle lived comfortable lives, too, but they never flaunted it. According to our parents, the three of us had bonded because of our "work ethics."

Now, I touched my saddle's name plate—a gift from my sister Charlotte. The brass plate read:

WHISPER
Lauren Towers

The ornamental satin brass tag had been Char's good luck gift to me. I ran my hand over the saddle's seat again, giddy. I'd only used it once before Canterwood to make sure the tree fit Whisper's back just right.

The saddle matched the equally gorgeous bridle with padded nose and brow bands. Both of my helmets hung above Whisper's saddle on pegs. I had a black Troxel helmet with a detachable visor for practice that was scraped and scratched from *plenty* of falls and a new Charles Owen

micro-suede covered helmet for shows. *That* one was in its own protective cover.

I carried my tack and helmet to Whisper's stall, resting everything on her trunk.

The mare's purple halter was on a peg next to her stall. I took it into the stall with me and her ears pointed forward. She knew what the halter meant!

I slipped the noseband over her muzzle and buckled the halter. I didn't need a lead line just to take her from the stall to crossties. With a light grip on the halter, I led her forward to the pair of crossties directly in front of her stall.

Honor's stall door was open, but I didn't see Lexa.

Whisper's ears swiveled and she sniffed the air, taking in her new surroundings as I clipped on the crossties. I stood beside Whisper's shoulder for a moment, stroking her until I was sure she seemed comfortable before walking to her tack trunk. I closed her stall door, put her saddle and pad over it, and draped her bridle across them.

I pulled open the heavy trunk lid. Inside, Whisper's gear was still arranged the way I'd painstakingly put it together. I loved looking at it all. The sets of bell boots, a winter blanket, lead lines, two leather halters, a tack box, shampoo, conditioner, and hoof polish were among some of the items I'd packed.

Whisper's tack box was *parfait*! The pale blue plastic matched the brushes and combs inside. And if I didn't want to carry the whole tack box, I had a mini Ariat carryall.

I put the box near Whisper and reached for a body brush. Whisper's coat, already mostly clean, just needed a light going-over. She grunted softly as I started near her poll and ran the brush down her neck. She enjoyed every second of it.

"Is this your version of a spa?" I joked. "It's time to do your hair and then your nails."

Whisper huffed at the sound of my voice. She was an excellent listener. All summer, I'd rambled to her about how nervous I was about Canterwood. One of her ears was always pointed in my direction and she'd make a different noise depending on what I told her. It was almost as if she'd been trying to assure me that she understood.

The wide-tooth comb slid easily through her mane. I'd thinned it the week before school started, so it took no time to comb. Whisper swished her tail playfully at me after I'd made it silky.

"Hey!" I patted her flank. "That's it for the hairstyling."

After I picked her hooves, I prepared to tack up. I reached for her saddle and suddenly found myself face-to-face with Riley.

 **93**

14

SNAP! JUDGMENT.

"WOW!" RILEY SAID, EYEING MY SADDLE. "That's *gorgeous*."

That was nice of her! I chided myself for making a snap judgment about Riley—especially on my very first day. Maybe we could be friendly after all.

"Thanks," I said, making sure to give her a genuine smile. "I worked for it all summer. My parents helped, though—it was their Welcome-to-Canterwood gift. Thanks for your compliment, Riley," I said. "It means a lot."

Riley widened her eyes. "Gosh," she said. "*My* parents offered to buy me a Butet, but I said no. I was too afraid the judges would think I'm one of those people who try to cover for their lack of skill with expensive tack."

Well, then, guess I'd been off on the whole "friendly" thing. I reminded myself that snap judgments were perfectly fine.

"Okay, then," I said politely, turning back toward Whisper.

"Oh, no," Riley said, holding up her hands. Her sincerity was about as authentic as a Chanel purse on Manhattan's Grand Street. "I definitely wasn't insinuating that *you're* a bad rider." She continued. "I mean, we *both* know a saddle isn't going to sway *Mr. Conner's* decision. You'd know that if you met Mr. Conner. Or maybe you *haven't*."

"Look," I cut in. "I didn't get this tack because it cost a lot of money." My voice was a notch lower than usual. "I work hard for everything. I. Get. Which is why I'm here— to work. So unless you actually have something useful to say . . . ?"

Riley looked as me as though I'd pointed out an enormous zit in the middle of her forehead. Her mouth was open, but nothing came out.

"Didn't think so," I said. "But thanks for stopping by!"

I turned around, scooped up the tack, and walked around to Whisper's side.

I heard Riley's boots clomp away. I smiled to myself.

Whisper's saddle pad fit smoothly on her back. I hoisted the saddle in the air, standing on my tiptoes. She was very tall at sixteen hands. She stood, patient, while I tightened the girth.

"Good girl," I said. "You know, you didn't meet her, but the last horse I rode filled her stomach with air sometimes. The saddle would be loose when I tried to mount her and then I'd slip sideways when she let the air out."

I peeked to make sure Riley was really gone . . . all clear. Phew! There were enough Rileys on the show circuit.

I shifted my full attention back to Whisper. I unhooked her crossties and slipped the reins over her head. Holding the crownpiece in my hand, I placed her snaffle bit in my hand. Whisper took it without hesitation and I put the crownpiece behind her ears and then buckled the bridle.

With a light hold on the reins, I put on my helmet.

"Time to go find Lexa," I told Whisper.

15

DON'T SCARE LT

WHISPER FOLLOWED ME DOWN THE AISLE, shoes clicking against the concrete. I didn't want to make Lexa wait long, but I couldn't help but slow a little to take in the beauty of the stable. The black iron bars gave the horses a wide view of the stable if their heads weren't poked out of the stall doors. Each stall was a roomy box stall with clean, deep sawdust. The wide, well-swept aisle had crossties every few stalls if a rider didn't want to tie his or her horse to iron bars.

Two stable grooms worked their way down the aisle, cleaning out stalls, refilling water buckets, and feeding horses.

I stepped out of the stable with Whisper on my heels. The sun had finally burned off the early morning fog and

I saw Lexa standing next to Honor. The horse reminded me of Ana's mare, Breeze, from a distance. A boy I'd never met stood next to Lexa. Whatever he'd just said made her laugh—her infectious laugh.

"Hey, Lauren," Lexa said when I reached them. "This," she said, slinging her arm over the taller boy's shoulder, "is Cole Harris. Cole is one of my best friends *and* he's a rider!"

"Don't listen to her," Cole told me, extending his hand to shake mine. He leaned in and whispered: "I'm *really* not a rider. I just love the clothes so much, I wear them here a lot and just hang out."

For a split second, I wasn't sure if it was a joke or not, but Cole smiled at me and Lexa shoved him saying, "Cole. We *like* LT. Don't scare her away, please?"

"Sorry, LT. It's nice to meet you."

"You, too," I said. "So, do you pleasure ride or are you on a riding team?"

"I made the intermediate team at the end of last year," Cole said. "I haven't been riding as long as most of the people here, but I'm trying to catch up."

"He's being modest," Lexa said. "He's a great rider. No catching up needed."

"I'm testing for a team," I said. "It feels a little intimidating. I'd love to see you ride sometime!"

Cole straightened his yellow polo shirt. "For sure. And don't stress the test. Mr. Conner's a *good* instructor. Lexa told me you guys are going on a trail ride, so she'll tell you everything you need to know. She's the best bestie a best bestie can have." His smile reached all the way up to his eyes.

"Back at you," Lexa said, bumping his arm with hers. She looked at me. "Cole not only made me a list of clothes to bring and new items to buy for school, but he also got on Skype with me and helped me put outfits together. He's a fashion genius."

"Oh, stop," Cole said. "I had to make sure you looked good so we could be seen together."

His green eyes sparkled. I loved the way they looked against his light brown hair.

Lexa laughed. "Seriously, he's going to be an amazing fashion designer. You should see his sketchbook someday. He's created some outfits that we're going to see in display windows one day. Dresses especially."

"We'll have to have talk fashion sometime," I said. "I'm obsessed with it. Especially classic looks."

"Have you sketched anything?" Cole asked.

"Not yet, but I'm taking fashion as my elective this year," I said. "I'm sure we'll be asked to draw."

"I'm taking fashion, too! Who's your teacher?"

"Ms. Snow," I said.

Cole smiled. "Awesome! Same class. It'll be fun."

"I'm glad to know someone already. I can't wait."

Cole checked his watch. "Sorry, girls, but I've got to run. I need to take care of Valentino and make sure he's settled in."

"See you," Lexa said.

"Bye," I said, smiling at him.

He walked toward the stable and I looked at Lexa.

"Cole's so nice," I said. "I didn't have any guy riders in my class at Briar Creek, but there seem to be lots of guys riding here."

"Definitely," Lexa said. "*Many* super hot ones."

Giggling, we mounted our horses.

We settled in our saddles and Lexa pointed toward woods that lined the back of the campus.

"Let's head that way," she said.

Whisper walked next to Honor, both mares bobbing their heads. Honor walked with confidence toward the woods. The activity of people riding, horses grazing in the pastures, and students laughing and moving from building to building didn't catch her attention.

Whisper's head moved from side to side—her eyes wide—as she absorbed the new surroundings. Tremors of

nerves rippled under her skin and I felt them through the saddle. I pushed my weight deeper into the seat and kept my legs light but firm against her sides.

Lexa observed us. "Whisper will be okay when we hit the trail. Honor did the same thing when we went out for the first time. She shrunk a little from all the activity, but she seemed to feel safe as soon as we were in the woods."

"Where's home?" I asked.

"Virginia."

"Have you always lived there?" We finally reached the start of the woods and, just as Lexa predicted, Whisper's taut muscles began to loosen.

"Same state, but two different cities," Lexa said. "My dad got a new job in D.C. a few years ago and we lived too far away for him to commute. We moved and I started riding for a great new stable."

"I got lucky, too, to come from a good stable before Canterwood. It gave me what I needed to get to Canterwood."

I didn't say what else I'd needed—self-confidence that I'd lost after my accident.

"I've heard about Briar Creek," Lexa said. "Everyone knows that's where Sasha Silver came from."

Sasha. The superstar equestrian whose shoes I'd been worried about filling. Worried there would be expectations of me to be as great as the legendary Sasha. But Kim and my parents had managed to convince me to make my own path.

"I didn't know her," I said. "I came to Briar Creek just after she came to Canterwood, I think. She and Charm are immortalized at Briar Creek. It's cool to come from the same town and stable that she did."

"Briar Creek is pretty small, right?" Lexa asked.

"Very small," I said. "A lot of riders do pleasure riding or the small-time show circuit."

I edged Whisper over so Lexa and Honor had enough room to skirt around a tree branch. The woods were gorgeous. The leafy trees allowed sunlight to filter through but still kept us cool. The well-worn dirt trail had lots to look at. Honeysuckle bushes flanked both sides of the trail. Giant bumblebees didn't even notice us as they zipped from flower to flower. Some of the trees had massive roots that snaked around the grass and down into the earth. The Connecticut air smelled fresh—full of possibility. Maybe . . . I had a chance at the intermediate team tomorrow.

"Thanks so much for bringing me out here," I said to Lexa. "I love it."

"I hoped you would. It's relaxing—my favorite thing to

do when I'm stressed or need to step away from campus."

"I'm a little nervous about testing tomorrow. Can you explain how it works?"

Lexa and I reached a clearing in the woods and we let the horses amble across the open field. The sun warmed my shoulders and glinted off Whisper's back. The field stretched for miles—never ending luxuriant grass. The horses acted more relaxed, too. Honor's ears flicked back and forth, waiting for a command from Lexa. Whisper's stride lengthened and she huffed out a slow breath.

"I'll tell you everything you need to know about testing. I might even tell you so much, you'll want me to stop."

I shook my head. "That will *not* happen! Talk away."

"Okay, so, you should have already gotten an e-mail from Mr. Conner with your testing time."

"Yep. Four-forty."

"You'll want to be at the stable as soon as you can after class. Get there early so you have plenty of time to spend with Whisper. I made sure I didn't just get to the stable, tack up, and warm up in the arena. I took a lot of time to talk to Honor. She kept me calm."

Lexa stood in the stirrups, leaned forward and scratched Honor's ear.

"I never like feeling rushed," I said. "That's definitely something I'll do. What time should I enter the arena?"

"Fifteen minutes before your test. Mr. Conner has all the riders scheduled with twenty minutes between them, so you can't go in too early. I would do the same warm-up you always do before a lesson."

I ran a hand over Whisper's shoulder. Talking about testing was scary, but each bit of advice from Lexa made it seem less daunting.

"Are other people watching besides Mr. Conner?" I asked.

"No," Lexa said. "It's a closed session. Mr. Conner won't ask you to perform any moves you haven't done before. He's not trying to trip up the riders—testing is about evaluating your current skills and deciding where those place you."

"That makes me feel better to know," I said. "I wasn't sure if he'd be asking for new things that I haven't done or haven't practiced much."

Lexa smiled. "I worried about that for my test last year. Hopefully, it'll help to know what's going on when you're there."

"I'll find a way to help you in return. Who else is already on the intermediate team?"

"Cole, Riley, Clare, Drew, and I are the current team. We're all new to it for this year. I'm so excited!"

"If I make the team, it will be so fun to ride with you. Cole, too. I know I only met him for a few minutes, but I really like him."

"Cole's the sweetest," Lexa said. "He and I were insta-BFFs when we met."

"He seems like the type of guy who gets along with everyone," I said. "And, like I said, it's nice to have guys at the stable."

"That's part of the reason why Cole's here," Lexa said, shaking her head. "He was bullied at his public school because he rode horses."

"*Cole?* Oh, my God."

"Some people at his old school thought riding was a 'girly' sport, and the bullying escalated the more Cole refused to fight back and sink to their level."

My mouth went dry. There had been a zero-tolerance policy regarding bullying at Yates. "How did it escalate?"

Lexa looked down then back at me. "It started with a couple of guys teasing Cole about riding. Then they picked on his clothes. One guy found his fashion sketchbook and tore out all the pages. He ripped them into pieces and threw them at Cole."

I tensed in the saddle and Whisper, feeling it, flicked an ear at me.

"Did Cole tell a teacher?"

"No. He wanted to handle it himself. But someone else must have seen it and reported it. Cole and the guy were called into the office. The bully got suspended for a few days."

"How did he treat Cole when he got back?"

Lexa pressed her lips together. "He thought Cole turned him in. He made Cole's life even more miserable."

"That makes me sick. It's disgusting that anyone would treat someone like that." Hearing Lexa talk about Cole's past made my stomach ache.

"It got worse from there," Lexa said. "Cole told me stories about guys shoving him up against lockers, writing mean things about him in bathroom stalls. Near the end, he was afraid to go to school. The guys threatened to beat him up."

I was silent for several seconds. It took me a moment to get the words out. "I can't imagine how Cole felt being treated like that. So that's why he came to Canterwood?"

"He applied because of the riding program, not because of the bullies. Cole told me he was going to stick it out and not let them run him out of school."

Wow. I sat back in my saddle. I didn't have Cole's courage. I wasn't even brave enough to be honest about my past.

"Once Cole got here, it took him a while to realize that he wouldn't be beaten up for saying he had riding practice after class," Lexa said. "Headmistress Drake doesn't tolerate bullying in any form, but from what I've seen—no one seems to care. There are lots of guy riders."

"I'm so glad Cole found a safe place," I said. "No one should be scared about going to school."

"Agreed," Lexa said. "Maybe think of Cole before your test. I do that when I'm scared, sometimes. Any more questions?"

"I think I'm set. Thank you so much for everything. And I won't repeat what you told me about Cole."

Lexa smiled. "You're welcome. And I didn't think you would. That's why I told you." She looked at me—a gleam in her dark eyes. "I think we all deserve a little more fun. Want to let the horses stretch with cantering then head back?"

"Absolutely!"

Simultaneously, we squeezed our legs against the horses' sides. Honor and Whisper moved into a trot, then a canter. Whisper's smooth strides ate up the ground. The pressure of testing slipped away with each stride.

16

DECORATORS, INC.

WHEN I GOT BACK TO MY ROOM A WHILE later, Khloe looked up from her copy of *Entertainment Weekly*. She'd changed from pj's to loungewear—a deep red velour track suit and a white V-neck T-shirt.

"Hey," she said. "I didn't even hear you leave."

"I'm glad I didn't wake you," I said, pulling off my paddock boots and putting them on our shoe rack. "I went out early so I could spend time with Whisper before it got hot. Now I've got the rest of the day to get ready for tomorrow."

Khloe looked at our room accessories and decorations in the corner. My eyes followed her gaze. "Want to do those?" she asked.

"Love to," I said. "I think it will make our room feel more like home when we get back from class."

"That definitely made me feel better last year," Khloe said. "And, believe it or not, the missing home feeling doesn't go away the second year. Decorating will make me feel good."

"Let me change out of my stable clothes and I'm game."

I changed into a white T-shirt with the Eiffel Tower and pink and lilac splotches. I paired it with black Pink shorts and pulled my hair into a messy bun. Mom had just started to let me shop from Victoria's Secret catalog Pink line. They had the cutest shirts, shorts, and pj's.

I tossed my riding clothes in my hamper and walked over to the corner where Khloe stood.

"Should we separate what we each brought and do inventory?" I asked.

"Good idea."

We carried our items to our beds, laying everything out. I stepped back, eyeing both beds and taking another survey of the room.

"I think everything's going to look great together," I said. "I'm so glad we coordinated our color scheme over the summer."

Khloe and I had traded a few e-mails to decide whose side of the room was going to be what color and what colors our shared items could be so they'd match. Luckily, Khloe's favorite color—light yellow—matched my light blue.

"Even more perfect that we're both Pottery Barn Teen addicts," Khloe said. "I have so many PBT catalogs in my room at home. I never throw them away. I swear my pile gets a little thinner every once in a while. I think my mom's sneaking them into the trash."

I laughed. "So, maybe we do the walls first? A few things need nails . . . are we allowed to do that or do we have to ask Christina?"

"Christina has to help," Khloe said. "But we can decide where we want to put them. You'll learn more of the rules at the Hawthorne orientation this afternoon."

"Totally forgot about that," I said.

At two, all of Hawthorne's seventh graders had to attend a mandatory orientation. Even returning students were required to go. I was glad Khloe and Lexa would be there.

"What do you think about putting the dry erase board on the wall by the end of my bed?" Khloe asked.

"Perfect spot." The whiteboard had adorable edging— pink with white dots.

"And the full-length mirror could go between my closet and the bathroom," I said.

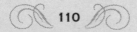

"Love!"

We went through item by item—making notes where we wanted to hang decorations that required nails.

The giant poster we'd both decided on—a hazy swirl of pink, blue, and yellow—went on the back of our door.

Over her bed, Khloe hung a black wire *K*. I put a framed collage of photos of my friends, Briar Creek, family, and Whisper above my bed.

Khloe added white wooden bookends to our bookcase. "I love them!" I said. One was the head, shoulders, and barrel of a horse. The other bookend was the hindquarters and flowing tail.

We'd both chosen peel-and-stick wall decals for our sides of the room. I'd picked bubble dot decals—different-sized circles of blue shades. I took my time placing them, overlapping some of the bubbles to make different shapes. Khloe had chosen bubble dots, too—hers were shades of pink. Moving them was easy and it changed the room's look in minutes.

Together, we'd picked out a pack of twenty tiny mini-butterfly mirrors. We put them over the counter in a cluster and they looked as if they were flying.

The violet-colored trash can went next to the edge of the counter, and we put organizers on the countertop

to hold straws, plastic cutlery, and other items we'd use often.

Khloe's desk was coming later today, so she put all of her desk accessories on the floor out of the way.

In the middle of the room, we put down a deep plush rug that matched the trash can. It covered most of the floor and went right up to the ends of our beds.

Khloe and I hung up our matching sheer curtains on white curtain rods. We replaced the boring knobs with clear ones with white swirls. The room looked *très magnifique!* My family and friends were going to love the pics. Becca was going to drool over the flat-screen TV mounted on the wall.

"Do you think we'll be able to assemble the coffee table?" I asked.

"I think so," Khloe said. "Hopefully, we just have to screw in the legs. I did that a lot this summer when my parents redid the living room."

We slid the heavy box to the center of the room, easing it down onto the floor. It was a gorgeous white table that we'd gone in on together. Khloe pulled out the instructions and we got started.

"Wow," I said. "You *were* good at that!"

Khloe grinned as we turned the table upright. I

grabbed a few pastel-colored coasters and scattered them on the table.

Lights were next. Together, we strung round, petal-pink mini paper lanterns across the tops of each of our windows and let a couple of excess lanterns hang down the sides. The tiny bulbs provided ultra-soft cozy lighting.

Khloe unboxed a tall, clear acrylic lamp with curves that spiraled toward the eggshell-colored shade with a soft yellow ribbon around the bottom. We found a spot for the lamp and, simultaneously, sighed.

"This. Looks. Amaze," Khloe said.

I held up my palm and we high-fived. "It's beautiful. I don't think we could have done any better if we'd hired a decorator."

"Ah-greed." Khloe looked at the wall clock we'd hung above the door—a simple but elegant silver clock. "And perfect timing—Christina's orientation in the common room is in five."

I followed Khloe out of our room and we headed down the hallway. The common room was packed—girls had already claimed every available spot to sit.

A voice, a notch louder than the rest, caught my attention. Riley sat in the center of the biggest couch with

Clare by her side. The girls around Riley stared up at her, nodding with every word she said.

Not exactly the dorm mate I'd hoped for. Khloe and I squeezed into the room along the back wall.

"Did you know Riley lived in Hawthorne, too?" I asked.

"Yes, unfortunately," Khloe said.

"Welcome, Hawthorne residents!" Christina's voice cut through the chatter. We all looked up to the front of the room.

Leaning my back against the wall, I took a closer look at the people in the room. It was like a chess game. Every girl in here seemed like she was positioning herself for something.

Maybe class president.

Top rider.

Most popular.

I wondered what, if anything, my label would become. I knew the one I didn't want—*ex-dressage champion.*

"My name is Christina," she said. "Some of you are new faces and others I recognize from last year." She smiled. "I'm not the kind of dorm monitor who's going to be watching your every move and making sure you're in class on time, going to bed at curfew, or not doing laundry for a month."

A couple of girls giggled.

"I *will* make sure your grades are on track, that you're in your rooms by the issued time and that no boys are in your rooms. The little things are up to you," Christina said. "You'll succeed or fail at Canterwood on your own. I'm placing your future in your own hands. I will be here, always, to support you, talk, or help in any way possible."

One word—*fail*—stayed in my brain. I couldn't fail. Not after everything it had taken to get here.

"I'm sure you all have things to do on your last day before classes start," Christina said. "I'd like each of you to grab a Hawthorne packet on your way out. Once you've finished reading it, sign and date the last page. There's a bin for them outside my office door. Your signature means that you agree to take responsibility for your future at Canterwood. If you're not serious about being here, don't sign it. Deal?"

We all nodded.

"That's it, then. I'm excited to kick off the new school year tomorrow! I look forward to getting to know the new students better and catch up with my girls from last year." Christina left the room, smiling.

Everyone moved to grab a packet. It was going to take Khloe and me forever from our spot at the back of the room. Riley stood and it was as if she had an electric field

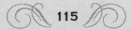

around her. Girls moved aside, many even ducking their heads, as Riley walked to the table with Clare on her heels.

"It's like the parting of the sea," someone muttered.

I turned and Lexa was beside me.

"No kidding," I said. "It's like she has magic powers."

Khloe rolled her eyes. "Riley has a big mouth. She never actually *does* anything, but she has a way with backhanded compliments and making competition a sport of its own."

"Khlo!" Clare reached her friend, her bouncing red curls sticking out in the crowd. "I *thought* I saw you back there with Lauren and Lex."

Clare handed Khloe three packets.

"Thanks. We would have been waiting forever," Khloe said. "Ooh, hey, Lauren and I just finished decorating our room." She looked at Lexa and Clare. "You guys want to come see?"

Clare's mouth opened and she paused, her eyes darting to the doorway. Riley stood there talking to a brunette I didn't know. "I would, but Riley's waiting. Sorry. I promised to go with her to The Slice."

"Okay, enjoy your pizza," Khloe said. "Maybe later?"

"Def," Clare said. "Bye." She disappeared after Riley.

Khloe turned to Lexa and me as if it didn't bother her, but I saw disappointment flicker in her eyes.

"I can't right now," Lexa said. "I'm meeting Jill and some friends from Orchard and Blackwell. But later for sure!" She frowned. "I'm sorry—I feel like I'm bailing on you after Clare blew you off."

"Clare didn't blow me off," Khloe said. "She—" Stopping, Khloe rubbed her temples. "I don't want to fight about Clare."

"Me either. Sorry, KK."

The girls smiled at each other and Lexa promised to come over when she was done hanging with her friends. Together, Khloe and I went back to our room.

The rest of the afternoon and evening went by fast—almost too fast. Khloe's desk arrived, we set it up together and then it was time for dinner. We ate and met up with Lexa who brought her roommate, Jill Carson, and they marveled at our room.

"Can I hire you two as our decorators?" Jill had asked. Lexa nodded in agreement.

I was proud that someone else liked our room. And proud that people were getting to know *me*.

Once alone again, Khloe and I changed into pj's, read and signed our packets from Christina. For a while, I texted Brielle and Ana while Khloe watched Disney's

Beauty and the Beast. My nervous energy took over and I organized and re-organized my binder for classes. I had everything sectioned off with colored tabs. Assignments. Schedule. Completed homework. Extra Credit.

When there wasn't anything left to rearrange, I pulled a mug from one of the cabinets. I wanted to make tea, but it was late—too late for me to leave our room. Instead, I stuck the mug of water inside our microwave and plucked a bag of Celestial Seasonings' Sleepytime tea from its box.

You really need to chill, I told myself. *But tomorrow is a huge day.* I shifted from foot to foot until the microwave beeped.

I dropped in the tea bag and stirred in a packet of Splenda. I put my mug on my nightstand and waited for the tea to steep. Khloe switched the movie to TV, pausing on a celebrity gossip channel.

"Did you hear that Annalynn and Tate broke up?" Khloe asked.

"No! They just got back together!" The sixteen-year-olds dominated box offices this summer with their romantic comedy and the gossip mags boasted that they'd taken their sizzling romance offscreen, too.

I leaned against my cozy pillow, not even realizing that my eyelids got heavier and heavier. I drifted off to sleep with my tea still steaming beside my bed.

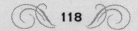

17

MONDAY MORNINGS SUCK

BEEEP! BEEEP! BEEEP!

Faint sunlight filtered through the curtains. I reached over and shut off the alarm, almost knocking over the cup of tea I hadn't gotten to touch last night before I fell asleep.

I'd had nightmares all night. The worst one had left me sweaty and gasping for air. I'd buried my head under the covers, trying to calm myself in the dark. If I'd been at home, I would have climbed into Becca's bed and she would have wrapped an arm around me until we both fell back asleep.

But Becca hadn't been there last night and it wasn't like I could wake Khloe.

The memory of the nightmare rushed back, making my heart beat a little faster.

I'd dreamed that I'd gone to my riding test. Instead of it being a closed session, every single rider from each grade filled the arena. Even Sasha Silver and her friends. Mr. Conner told me that I couldn't test. I asked him why and he said, "You may still be Lauren Towers, but you're not the rider you used to be."

Out of nowhere, a giant TV appeared and footage I recognized all too well started to play. I was riding at the Red Oak Horse Trial. The announcer called my name and my mount's—Skyblue.

I begged Mr. Conner to stop the footage from playing, but it was if he didn't hear me.

No one heard me.

They didn't pay attention to anything but Lauren on the TV.

"Lauren," Mr. Conner said. "You can't keep secrets at Canterwood."

Once I'd woken up, it had taken me hours to get back to sleep, and when I finally had, it was almost time to get up.

I looked at Khloe. She was sprawled on her bed, one of her tan legs dangling off the side. She'd set her own alarm to get up later, so I didn't wake her.

I hopped into the shower, lathering my long hair with

Bumble and bumble shampoo. The coconut-scented kind was my favorite. I rinsed, applied conditioner, and combed it through my hair before clipping it up. Once a week or just before special occasions, I let conditioner stay on my hair for a few extra minutes to make it as soft and shiny as possible. It was an EBT—essential beauty tip—that Brielle had taught me.

I squeezed vanilla-scented body wash into my loofah sponge and scrubbed down to my toes. Once I finished my shower, I wrapped my hair in a towel and got dressed. The shower felt as though it washed away all the remnants and worries of last night.

Now I was ready to focus on today. First thing this morning, Headmistress Drake was holding a meeting in the auditorium.

After that, I had math. At least I was looking forward to that—Khloe and Lexa were in my class.

Khloe hadn't moved an inch since I'd showered. I giggled. Khloe had really meant what she'd said about sleeping until the last possible minute.

I took inventory of my reflection in the mirror. One pale blue T-shirt with a tiny pocket. One flowy black knee-length skirt. And silver ballet flats with ruffles around the edges. I'd picked out my outfit the night before as usual.

I unwrapped my hair and misted it with Bb Prep. I'd gone simple with accessories—tiny white-gold diamond studs and a matching necklace with a letter *L* dangling from a thin chain.

I microwaved a cup of hot water and made white pear tea for a little boost. I didn't want to have green tea—I already had enough energy.

I picked up my BlackBerry and opened my Chatter application to post a quick message.

LaurBell: Getting ready 4 1st day @ Canterwood! So nervous.

At my desk, I set up my makeup mirror and pulled out my bag from Sephora. The Canterwood handbook didn't restrict seventh graders from wearing makeup, but it *did* say that we weren't allowed to wear makeup or clothes that were "distracting."

Khloe's alarm, her iPod plugged into a dock, suddenly started to play an upbeat morning mix. Khloe swiped at the snooze button and missed.

"Argh!" she grumbled. She hit the clock and silenced the music. She fell back into bed.

Biting my lip to keep from giggling, I rubbed tinted moisturizer with sunscreen onto my face then applied a light dusting of champagne-colored eye shadow over my lids. Finally, I rubbed Smith's Rosebud salve over my lips,

and used my angled brush to sweep a shimmery peach blush over my cheeks.

My phone beeped and a smiley face icon lit up on my screen. I had a Chatter reply.

BrielleisaBeauty: @LaurBell U r going 2 do GREAT, LT! ♥ *u!*

I wrote her back and included Ana.

@BrielleisaBeauty: Hope so! I miss u guys! Have a good 1st day @ Yates! @AnaArtiste

Khloe's music started again and, finally, groaning, she sat up. She brushed back her long hair and turned off the alarm.

"Monday mornings suck," Khloe grumbled.

"Would coffee or tea help?" I asked.

Khloe smiled, rubbing her eyes. "Thanks, but I'm okay. We'll grab breakfast at the cafeteria—you don't have to get me anything."

"Okay," I said. "But I *am* a morning person. So if you ever want anything in the morning, let me know."

"Thanks, I will," Khloe said, getting out of bed and stretching. I loved her Xhilaration pj's from Target—dark blue pants with multicolored dots and a hot-pink tank top with lace straps. "Do you need the bathroom? If not, I'm going in."

"Nope," I said. "I'm going to dry my hair out here in front of the big mirror."

While Khloe got ready, I dried my hair—taking my time to section it off and use a round brush to leave it smooth but wavy. I decided to leave it natural today—no flatiron.

I couldn't stop thinking about what could happen today. I vacillated between being nauseous-slash-nervous and excited-slash-terrified. I turned off the dryer and saw a fully dressed Khloe waving at me.

"Do you want to set your hair on fire?" she asked, her tone light. "You've been drying that section for a while."

"Really?" I touched my hair and it almost burned my fingertips. "Oops. Thanks, Khlo. Must be nerves."

Khloe walked over. "Your hair looks great."

"Thanks. Just a little more drying and—"

"Lauren." Khloe cut me off and touched my arm. "It's okay to be scared. Now, let's stop drying your hair before it fries, put on your shoes, and then we'll grab our bags and go. I know what you're feeling—I was *beyond* nervous."

"But you're so outgoing! I can't imagine you scared."

"When I'm onstage or playing a character, it's easy to be like that. But when I'm just Khloe Kinsella, I'm not anyone who I portray onstage. I'm anxious about this morning, too. Even though it's my second year, classes are new and it's like everything is reset to zero. I have to do things all over again, too, like getting used to the fast pace of Canterwood . . . and readying for my audition on Friday."

Khloe gently took the hair dryer away from me and placed it on the desk. "I just want you to know that I'll be there for you today. You can always BBM me even if you just have a question or want to say hi. Okay?"

"Thanks, Khloe. That makes me feel a *lot* better. It's weird—I've changed schools a bunch of times. But Canterwood feels so overwhelming. I *really* want to do well and fit in."

"You will," Khloe said. "You've already got Lexa and me. I think you and Jill will get along really well, too. Everyone in our grade is going to like you. It'll be the same at the stable; Lexa introduced you to Cole, so you already know one more person there!"

I nodded.

Khloe's brown eyes were so sincere. After knowing me for a weekend, she was already trying to comfort me and be a good friend. Guilt settled into my stomach. *You should have told her this weekend about your competition past,* I scolded myself.

Khloe was my roommate and fast becoming my friend—she didn't deserve to have someone keeping a giant secret from her. I even *wanted* to tell her—I just wasn't ready quite yet. It had taken me a long time of getting to know Ana and Brielle before I'd even told them.

I realized I hadn't answered Khloe. "Um . . . y-you're right," I stammered. "I do know people, and I will definitely BBM you if I need to."

"You better." Khloe smiled. "Let's get to the assembly."

I put on my ballet flats and picked up my bag. And Khloe slung her leather satchel over her shoulder, a spiral notebook in her arms.

Together, we walked down the hallway in Hawthorne with other students around us. I felt as though I could breathe a little better after Khloe's pep talk.

"Does Canterwood provide a rolling cart for us to carry all of our books?" I said, only half joking. "It feels like I've got bricks in my bag."

"If only," Khloe said. "But you can swing by our room between classes if you have time."

I thought about how strange that would be—how strange it was to be at boarding school in general.

Khloe and I walked to the auditorium full of students. A few plush red seats were left. The huge stage had a microphone stand set up front and center. Red curtains were raised, and I glanced around at all the lights. The room was huge. Cherubs had been carved into the beautiful cherry wood moldings.

"How many grades are here now?" I asked Khloe, still in awe.

"Seventh and eighth." Khloe said, scanning the room. Someone waved; I could only see an arm. "There's a separate auditorium for the high school."

"Wow," I exhaled.

"Lexa and Jill are over there," Khloe said. "Bet they prob saved us seats!"

We walked down the aisle, the stairs well lit by the overhead lights and ropes of lights along each side.

"Excuse me," Khloe said as we entered the aisle where Lex and Jill sat. We made our way past a few students, trying not to step on toes or backpacks. There were two empty seats—one beside Lexa and the other next to Jill.

Jill had her shoulder-length, light brown hair in a low side ponytail that had been curled at the end by a curling iron. Jill's hair was *très* chic. Plus, I *loved* the pretty spray of freckles across her nose. She wore black-plastic-framed glasses (*très belle!*) that drew attention to her bright green eyes.

"Thanks for saving us seats," I said, walking past Lex and taking the seat next to Jill. Khloe settled in the seat by Lexa.

"No prob," Jill said. "I got here first. Lex couldn't find one of her books, so she told me to go without her."

The auditorium lights dimmed as the collective noisy conversations simmered to occasional whispers as Headmistress Drake walked up the stairs, her heels clicking across the wooden floor. My smile brightened as I caught a flash of the vibrant red on the unmistakable Louboutin heels. Headmistress Drake looked all business in a black skirt, blazer, and white shirt. A gold pin with the school's crest gleamed on her lapel. Her shiny black hair was chopped in a stylish bob.

"Good morning," she said. "Welcome to a new year at Canterwood Crest Academy."

18

SECOND CHANCES DON'T EXIST

THE HEADMISTRESS'S WORDS GAVE ME goose bumps. She stood before me, seeming to see each and every student in the room.

"Each of you, returning or new, is here because you were accepted to an institution with the highest of standards," Headmistress Drake said. "As is done at the beginning of each academic year, I would like to take this opportunity to read aloud the Canterwood Crest Academy conduct code and policy agreement. This will ensure that all of you know what is expected of you by your instructors, your peers, and all of the Canterwood Crest community, including faculty and staff, alumni, and of course, myself."

This was serious. There was no hint of a smile on the

headmistress's face. Her firm tone was enough for me to vow *never* to end up in her office.

Ever.

For *any* reason.

"Your commitment to excellence began the moment you walked through these doors." Headmistress Drake pointed toward the double doors at the back of the auditorium. She continued. "Collectively, the people sitting in this room today—and those who have sat here in the years, decades, and generations before you, have dedicated themselves to building a reputation that is regaled and respected nationwide. We pride ourselves on students who are now and have always been committed to academic excellence, and who strive to inspire fellow leaders throughout our great country and beyond.

"Our students are human beings who take advantage of opportunity."

As Drake paused to sip from her rectangular bottle of Fiji water, it occurred to me that there was no giggling, no note passing that I could see, no rolling of eyes. Every single student—including me—was held rapt. Hanging on every last word.

"As I was saying," Drake said, "upon completion of your journey at Canterwood Crest Academy, you find"—she

paused to smile—"the world will be your oyster. The metaphorical pearl at its center, the rare but beautiful stone, is the Academy—the place that made you who you are. The very institution that gave you every tool, every key, you'll ever need to unlock the door through which one achieves greatness in any and every one of life's endeavors.

"And all that we ask in return is that you treat your school and, however temporary, your *home* with the care and respect that pearl, that elusive key to greatness, deserves."

There was a *whoosh* while all the seventh- and eighth-grade students jumped to their feet, and then a deafening roar of applause. Those who could, showed off their two-fingers-in-the-mouth whistling trick.

I was stunned.

During the applause, Khloe reached past Lexa *and* Jill to squeeze my hand and smile at me. Her smile, though I'd only just met her, was easy for me to read. It said, *These are going to be the best and scariest years of your life, and you're going to love. Every. Minute.*

The second squeeze was easier to read and told me something I suddenly realized I wanted with all my heart.

It said, *And I'm going to be there the whole time if you want me there.*

I smiled, nodded, and squeezed back. *Yes!*

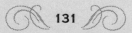

"Okay, have a seat," Drake said. In an instant we all sat, and the room was silent once again. "I trust you *all* have read the updated handbook and are familiar with our rules and regulations." Headmistress Drake's face was no longer smiling or friendly. "There will be no grace period for broken rules. You have had all summer to familiarize yourself with the codes of conduct.

"All your teachers expect full participation in class," she continued. "Your dorm monitors expect their rules to be followed, and *I* expect students to represent my school with model behavior. If you are not able to fulfill these obligations, or those in the handbook, you *will* be sent home. No exceptions. Zero second chances."

The last sentence made my stomach flip-flop. I knew all the rules and had never been in trouble at school before, but what if I messed up somehow?

"Yikes," Jill whispered to me. "She will never *not* scare me."

I was too scared to say anything back.

Headmistress Drake smiled. "With that said, I have no doubt that you will all put forth your best effort this year. I look forward to seeing those of you who have returned. For new students, I'm extremely proud that you chose Canterwood as your school. I can't wait for

you to get to know Canterwood. And I can't wait for our community at Canterwood to get to know *you*. And now . . . you are all dismissed. Your first-period teachers are waiting!"

I let out a breath I didn't realize I'd been holding.

Headmistress Drake exited the stage, and there was a flurry of activity. Bags of every color (and, I noticed, high-end *labels*) were hoisted over shoulders as students raced for the exit doors. I hurried after Lexa, Khloe, and Jill.

"Guess no one wants to be late to the first class of the year?" I asked.

"Not after that speech!" Jill said, laughing. It had been like a stampede. No joke.

Khloe, Lexa, and I waved good-bye to Jill from the courtyard as she headed to her class and we went to math. The math building wasn't far from the courtyard, but a little anxiety washed over me as we stepped into the air-conditioned building and walked down the tiled hallways to room 107.

A desk and giant whiteboard were in the front of the huge classroom. The rows of individual desks didn't have names on them, so Lexa found three desks together and Khloe slung her beautiful pink Coach purse adorned with oversized iridescent sequin piping over the back of the

one in the middle. Lex sat in front of her, and I happily took the desk next to Lexa.

I glanced around as seats filled.

I wanted to be ready before the teacher came in, so I turned around and reached into my messenger bag. I pulled out my textbook, a new spiral notebook labeled MATH and a pen. Something was missing . . . *calculator*.

When I turned around to fish it out of my bag, my arm knocked my pencil to the ground. I leaned over to pick it up at the same time the guy beside me did. He got it first.

"Here you go," he said, giving me a very sweet (read: *cute*) smile. His shaggy-chic blond hair was side-swept out of his eyes but still lingered past his eyebrows.

"Thanks," I said, taking the pencil from him. I started to reach for my calculator again.

"Did you just transfer?" Pencil Guy asked. His red-headed friend turned and shot me a smile, too.

"That obvious, huh?" I asked. "So, the pencil dropping and terror-filled eyes gave me away?"

Both boys laughed.

"Gotcha," I said. "Next time I'll bring a pen to class."

"I don't think that would help," the blonde said. He leaned toward me like he was telling me a secret. "It's a small class, so we know everyone here. I'm Zack, and that's my friend—"

"Garret," Garret broke in.

"Lauren," I said. "Nice to meet you guys." This felt good. Right. Like something I would have done at Yates if I'd met two new guys. I was never supershy—I often had more guy friends than girlfriends no matter what school I was at.

"Khloe."

I looked away, toward the unfriendly voice. Riley stood, smiling down at Khloe. Her supershiny dark hair was back in a French braid. She'd somehow done her eyeliner in a flawless cat-eye that was superflattering. She'd paired dressy black shorts with charcoal-gray-and-black horizontal-striped tights and a black scoop-neck tee with silver stitching. Poison-red peep-toe ballet flats completed the look. "The look" being . . . well, perfect.

Her liquid brown eyes swept over me. "Lauren. And Lexa. Wow, and *Khloe.* Aren't you three just the cutest fast besties?"

Riley walked past me, her black butter-leather Chanel bag almost sweeping everything off my desk. I inspected the stitching as the bag grazed my belongings. *Be a knockoff, be a knockoff,* I chanted silently—and irrationally. But the stitching was barely visible and *parfait.*

Why did girls like Riley always have the real-deal Chanels? And why did this particular Chanel owner have to sit directly behind *me*?

There was a light tap on my shoulder. I pasted a sickly sweet smile onto my face before turning to look at Riley.

"I'm sorry if I interrupted your conversation," she said, glancing at the guys. Zack and Garret had started talking to a third boy—the three of them laughing about something.

"No big," I said honestly. "I had a very small clumsy moment and they gave me an intro."

I tried smiling at Riley, but I could feel my smile coming off as frowny.

Riley apparently had a smiling problem, too. "It's so great that you have *friends* on the first day, social butterfly. Let me guess—you're sharing stories about tiny town life that everyone thinks is *so* quaint and adorable?"

"Weird!" I said. "It's like you're inside my *brain*." I plucked my calculator from my bag and put it on my desk.

"Here are those directors you asked for," Lexa said, folding a piece of paper into my hand.

Huh? I opened the paper slowly.

Here's my #. BBM urs 2 KK & me so we can talk w/o Riley hearing. Ohhh. Ha!

I slid my phone onto my lap and BBMed Lexa and Khloe my number.

Khloe: LT! u talked 2 Zack! & Garret!

Lexa: & made Reiler look like the brat she is!

Lauren: Reiler? Ugh. Not a fan. ?? abt Zack and Garret?

Khloe: 2 of the hottest guys in r class! What did u say 2 them? (& Reiler = Rottweiler.)

Lauren: Oh! Nothing 2 get excited abt—trust me. He just intro'd himself & G. LOL re: Reiler. ♥

Simultaneously, Lexa and Khloe wrote: *OMG!*

Lauren: Srsly! U guys r so funny.

Khloe: Z or G prob would have asked u out if R hadn't walked in.

Our teacher walked into the classroom and I smiled at Khloe and Lexa, shaking my head. I locked my phone and shoved it in my bag.

"Welcome, class. I'm Ms. Utz," the teacher said.

Ms. Utz was 6'5 tall and muscular—like she could bench-press her desk. Her blue-black hair was pulled into a bun so tight it must have given her a headache. She didn't wear any makeup except for lip balm.

Ms. Utz counted out handouts for each row and gave them to the first person in each one.

"Before we begin new concepts," Ms. Utz said, "let's use today as a refresher. Once we begin this year's lessons, there

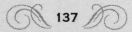

will not be time to go back. If after today's class there is a concept you've either forgotten or have not fully mastered, I strongly suggest you come see me or seek tutoring."

I sat up a little straighter. I'd gotten As in math from Yates. *But this isn't Yates.*

"Please close your textbooks, put your notebooks under your desks, and leave out only a pencil," Ms. Utz said. "A pop quiz is the easiest way to judge your skill level."

Scattered groans erupted across the classroom.

Ms. Utz smiled. "I must be doing my job right if I can make you all groan on the very first day." She grinned—showing off bright white square teeth.

Lexa passed a quiz back to me and I handed the last one to Riley.

"You have half an hour," Ms. Utz said. "You may begin . . . now."

I put down my pencil just as Ms. Utz called, "Time." I'd actually finished a couple of minutes early and had been rechecking my work.

Ms. Utz picked up each student's paper. Surprisingly, I felt good about my quiz. I'd gotten stuck on a few problems, but I used my usual strategy—I left them blank and

moved through the rest of the quiz. After I finished, I came back to the problems I skipped.

Ms. Utz spent the few remaining minutes of class telling us what to expect of the semester, going through the syllabus and answering questions. Once the bell sounded, Ms. Utz told us to enjoy the rest of our first day. Tough as she looked, I had a feeling I would like my new math teacher.

Lexa, Khloe, and I walked out together and escaped from the building without any more "Reiler" encounters.

"First class down!" Lex said, smiling at me.

"First class down," Khloe said. "And *you*"—she grinned at me—"met two supercute boys."

"Stop!" I laughed. "They were being polite—that's *all*."

"Ohhh, *polite*! Just like a seventh-grade boy. Okay, LT," Lexa said in a singsong voice.

I smiled to myself.

Honestly, at all my old schools, I'd always gotten along with pretty much everyone. Being an athlete gave me something in common with the boys who played sports. That's how I'd bonded with Taylor. Ana, Brielle, and I hadn't been exclusive or cliquey. Everyone, except for a few catty girls, got along with us. It seemed as if Khloe, Lexa, and Jill were pretty cool.

Maybe they'd even earn the Ana and Brielle SOA—stamp of approval.

As we headed for Mr. Spellman's history class, I couldn't help but think that *maybe*, just maybe, I could do this.

19

SOMEONE'S A LITTLE *TOO* COMFY

BY THE TIME I ENTERED THE CAFETERIA, MY bag was weighed down with more homework and handouts than my first *week* at Yates. Khloe had forgotten her Canterwood meal card, so she and Lexa had run back to Hawthorne to get it.

I got in line with my tray, thinking about the past two classes. History with Mr. Spellman had been fun. He was a little odd but in a funny, endearing way. Quirky, not creepy. He hadn't quizzed us or given us a ton of homework for tonight. All we had to do was read the first chapter in our textbook, which covered American history before 1500. Which, by the way, our textbook? Had our teacher's *name* in it as one of the contributors. No kidding—it was like meeting someone famous. He didn't even *tell* anyone.

And when I told Khloe about the textbook thing, she just stared at me without speaking for a long time, then said, "Cool. My teacher literally wrote a book on the most boring subject ever." Then she continued to grumble about reading "boring stuff" on our way to English. Not that it was my favorite time period either, but still. The guy rated miniceleb on my scale.

When I asked him about the name after class, he actually turned red! If it had been me teaching the class? I'd be like, "Please turn to the *cover* of this book and notice that *I wrote things in here.* We don't have to dwell on it, but you should definitely acknowledge that I'm very smart and my name being in print proves it. That will be all. Class dismissed."

I mean, I knew Canterwood teachers were "top-notch educators from all over the world." The brochures talked about that almost as much as their "extremely accomplished alumni" who have "gone on to discover very important scientific" . . . well, discoveries. Not to mention the alumni who had "seats" in very important government positions. So far, however, I was most impressed by current students like Sasha Silver, who I still looked for everywhere I went, and my weirdly hyper and modest history professor who HELPED WRITE OUR

TEXTBOOKS!!! Not that Yates's professors weren't intimidatingly smart. But this whole day had been like a dream.

At first, English had been a little tense. And *not* because of the teacher. Clare had walked in after Khloe and I had found seats. Khloe had waved her over, and Clare had sat next to her. They'd started talking immediately, and I'd given them some space and stayed low profile. But Khloe, seemingly not to want me to feel excluded, pulled me into a convo about our cute teacher.

Khloe and Clare had already seen him in person—I'd only seen photos on the CCA website. Without Riley, Clare acted like a different person. She and Khloe were closer than I'd seen them, and I could tell Clare was really making an effort to be friendly with me.

When Mr. Davidson had walked in, Khloe and Clare had turned to me with total *Told you so!* looks on their faces. Mr. Davidson was definitely even cuter in person than he was in his online pic. Even *Khloe* (!) had blushed or stammered when he'd called her name for attendance.

He was a lot younger than most of the teachers. *And* his dashing blue eyes, thick wavy hair, and classic, all-American, Ralph Lauren sense of style made him look like a movie star. Mr. Davidson had simply gone over the syllabus, promising to explain in greater detail tomorrow.

Posters of black-and-white photographs of famous authors covered the classroom walls. The desks were arranged in a circle. Both so we could see each other *and* because open discussion was encouraged, he'd told us.

Mr. Davidson was so nice, he'd even apologized for giving us homework on the first day: reading about memoirs in our textbook and writing a three-to-five-page piece about the most important things we actually wanted him to know about us.

"Your turn," someone said behind me.

I was holding up the entire lunch line behind me with my daydreams.

"Sorry!" I said, hurrying up to the lunch lady. "I'd like a turkey sandwich on whole wheat bread, carrots with a side of blue cheese dressing, a strawberry cupcake, and iced tea, please."

She put the items on my tray and swiped my meal card.

The caf was *massive*. Long tables. Small square tables. Round tables. Corner tables. Sunlight streamed in through numerous windows. Instead of fluorescent lights like the ones in Yates's cafeteria, Canterwood had spaced-out lights—simple white balls—that hung down from the ceiling on slender silver poles and provided warm lighting.

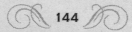

I scanned the room for a good table. One near a window that faced the gym was open. I put down my tray and slid onto the seat, putting my bag beside my feet. I opened BBM.

Lexa: KK and I will b right there. Save us seats! ☺

Lauren: Done! Table nxt 2 window on left side.

There was also a message from Taylor. Seeing his name on my phone was still bittersweet. We'd had the best breakup possible (mutual), and I was lucky that we'd been able to stay friends. But sometimes I wasn't so sure. Sometimes I missed him as more than a friend.

I opened the message he'd sent an hour ago. Then the ones from Bri, Ana, and Becca.

Taylor: How's the 1st day? I keep expecting 2 run into u here. Okay, so that made my heart deflate a little.

Brielle: TT, how is the fabulous CC? A & I miss r BFF!

Ana: Laur-Bell, Yates is totally boring w/o u. Srsly. Oh, Jeremy says hi!

I smiled at the mention of her BF—an artist, too, of course.

I looked at the message from Becca: *How is it all, Laur? BBM me—keeping fingers crossed all day 4 u. Love u.*

I stuffed my phone in my bag and bit my lip. I busied myself with my iced tea.

"Hey!" Khloe slid into the seat across from me. "I'm starving."

"Me too," said Lexa, sitting next to Khloe.

"I'm never this hungry at lunch," I said. "But it feels like I've been running mini marathons between classes."

"We kind of have been," Khloe said, taking a gulp of chocolate milk.

Lexa took a bite of her chicken sandwich. "It's going to take weeks before I'm used to this schedule again."

"Rushing between buildings should so count as gym," I said, holding up a declarative pointer finger. "I've got French III, gym, and science left still. I might actually *die* during gym." Okay, so maybe Khloe was rubbing off on me.

"Ms. Meade," Lexa said, "Lauren couldn't make it to class. She died doing push-ups."

We all laughed and began eating at an embarrassingly rapid rate. Manners? Gone. No one even *spoke* until our trays were empty.

"Ugh," Lex said. "I ate too fast."

I rubbed my stomach. "Yeaaah. I don't even remember eating my cupcake."

"So who has what left?" Khloe asked.

"Spanish, history, and science," Lexa said.

"I have Spanish, science, and acting," Khloe said. "That means one class doesn't count."

"At least you guys have Spanish together," I said. "And Lexa and I have science."

"Acting isn't even like a real class, so I just have to get through science," Khloe said.

"Spanish will be . . . ," Lex said, "well, we don't have the best track record with that."

"*Sí,*" Khloe said, giggling.

It hit me at that moment: three more classes and I was done. I'd go back to my room, change, and walk to the stable. At 4:40 I'd be in the arena in front of Mr. Conner. I'd been too overwhelmed all day to think about testing. Now that I was sitting still, anxiety pumped through me.

From the day I'd been accepted to Canterwood, I'd told myself over and over that I'd feel proud even just to be on the school's beginner team. But deep down I knew I was lying to myself. I wanted more. I wanted to make the intermediate team.

"You three are just bonding away over here."

Riley sauntered up to us, jutting out a bony hip when she stopped.

"What's up?" Khloe asked, her tone fake-cheery. And

we all know that Khloe could have done better if she wanted.

"I wanted to stop by and see how Lauren was feeling," Riley said, her concern as false as Khloe's excitement to see her.

"About what?" I asked. This girl was really starting to grate on me.

"Testing." Riley's eyes widened. "You didn't forget, did you?"

"Of course, no. But I'm doing just fine. Thank you so much for your concern."

"*Well.* I'm glad you're feeling so confident," Riley said. "I've seen some riders so nervous they can't even eat before testing. But you don't seem worried one bit. To top it off, you flirted with Zack and Garret on your very first day! That's major."

The girl was so odd. Why did she want to argue with *me*, of all people? It wasn't like I was competition to her. So why did she like twisting everything I said and did? Still, I wasn't going to give her the pleasure. I wouldn't argue with her. It wasn't worth the energy.

"Zack and Garret?" I asked. "Huh. I never thought of it. Well, I'll get their numbers and see if they're free this week. Maybe do pizza with Zack one night. Maybe

a movie with Garret the next." I shrugged, holding up both palms as though I were carrying a tray of pies in each hand. "Who knows? Life can be *so strange*."

Riley's eyes widened. I made eye contact with Khloe— holding her gaze for a second. She must have understood, because she slid her elbow into Lexa's arm. Riley was in too much shock to even notice. If looks could kill, I'd have been sipping tea with Coco Chanel and my Gran Hazel by now. But I was still here, so I looked right at Riley and drained my iced tea. "Right?!" I said.

Riley's phone chimed three times before she remembered to close her mouth—and that it wasn't polite to stare. She took her phone from her pocket and frowned. "I have somewhere to be," Riley nearly spat. She walked over to her nearby table and grabbed her tray and bag. She was halfway across the caf before a confused Clare had time to hurry after her friend. But Riley had long since exited the caf.

"That," Khloe said, "was the *best*! She had no clue what to do with you."

"*No* clue," Lexa agreed. "You might be my new personal hero."

I giggled with Khloe and Lexa. "So does that mean," I asked, "you'll help me plan my dates with Zack and Garret?"

"We'll do you one better," Khloe said. "Your hair and makeup. I bet Zack prefers beachy waves. And for Garret?"

"Flatiron?" We all said at once. The three of us laughed.

At least I'd told Riley the Reiler one very true thing: I was beginning to feel very comfortable thanks to two people I hoped I'd always call my friends: Khloe and Lexa.

20

EXCUSEZ-MOI?

"BONJOUR," MME. LAFLEUR SAID.
"Bienvenue á la classe de français!"

"Merci," the class said together.

Mme. LaFleur turned around to the whiteboard and
uncapped a blue marker.

Je m'appelle Madame LaFleur.

She glanced back at the class and nodded at a girl in
the first row. *"Comment vous appelez-vous?"*

I relaxed a little. I'd expected to walk into French III
and have the teacher speak entirely in French, not use
a word of English for the entire period, and lose me in
translation. Instead, Mme. LaFleur started off easy by
asking each of us our names.

"Je m'appele Jordan," the girl said.

"Enchanté," Mme. LaFleur said.

Mme. LaFleur looked to the student behind Jordan. She started to ask the same question when the classroom door opened.

"Je suis désolé," Riley said. *"Je m'appele Riley."*

Mme. LaFleur folded her arms, listening to the apology.

"I was in the cafeteria," Riley continued. "One of the lunch staff dropped a stack of trays with food. I couldn't just walk around them and leave them to clean it all themselves. Again, I'm incredibly sorry. And no, I didn't want to make any excuses—I'm late. It won't happen again."

I raised an eyebrow. No way would Mme. LaFleur buy Riley's lame lunch lady story.

"Non, Riley. C'est très bonne. Merci pour ton assistance," Mme. LaFleur said. *"Maintenant, s'il vous plaît."* She gestured toward an empty seat.

"D'accord," Riley said. *"Merci."*

She hooked her Chanel over the back of the chair. The second Riley's back was to Mme. LaFleur, she smirked right at me.

For the rest of the period, I didn't glance in Riley's direction once.

Mme. LaFleur explained what we'd be learning throughout the semester and we went over a few intermediate phrases that had become a little rusty for me over the summer. My head stayed bent over my desk as I took copious notes.

Mme. LaFleur dismissed us at the end of the period without any homework—win!—and I was one of the first students out the door, leaving Riley behind. *Are you going to let her run you out of the room after every class you share?* I asked myself as I slowed in the hallway.

The answer came immediately: *N-O-N.*

I was in autopilot all through gym. In my gym uniform— hunter green shorts and a white T-shirt—I made a lap around the outdoor track, stretched, and did whatever else Coach Warren told our class to do.

Riley and Clare were in gym with me, but they stuck together and left me alone. Testing had me so preoccupied; I didn't even realize until I left to change that the guy I most definitely was *not* crushing on from the Sweet Shoppe—Drew—had been in my class.

That pulled me out of my haze a little. I tried to remember if I'd done anything embarrassing during class. Not that it was important. I wasn't interested in boys right

now—school and riding would be my two true loves . . . at least until the end of first semester.

But for those few minutes I thought about Drew, I stopped thinking about testing.

21

BBM, SET, GO!

AFTER SCIENCE CLASS, I RACED OUT OF THE building and through the campus to Hawthorne. Science hadn't held my attention, either. Nothing would right now.

Lexa had been in the class with me and I liked Ms. Meade, but my focus was *gone*. I promised myself I'd pay extra attention to the science syllabus tonight.

Khloe wasn't in the room when I got there. She'd had something to do but said she'd be at the stable waiting for me when I finished testing. I yanked off my school clothes and slipped into breeches and a grape-colored T-shirt with light gray stripes. I redid my ponytail then turned on the faucet, splashing cold water on my cheeks.

If I rode Whisper while I was this nervous, she would pick up on it. *Calm down and breathe.*

I put on socks and tall black boots, all the while telling myself: *You'll feel better the second you see Whisper.*

I forced myself to walk at a normal speed to the stable and even posted a Chatter update while I walked: *LaurBell: Going 2 test 4 CCA's riding team. *gulps** Okay, that didn't help.

At the stable, it was much quieter than it had been over the weekend. The tack room was empty. I looked at Whisper's tack. It wasn't even close to being dirty, but it wasn't gleaming either, and everything had to look perfect when I rode for Mr. Conner.

I checked the time on my BlackBerry. There was plenty of time to wipe down the saddle and bridle, but I admonished myself—I should have done it earlier. Certainly not the day of testing!

I grabbed a soft cloth from a communal bin of rags and sponges for tack cleaning. Instead of deep cleaning with oil, I sprayed the cloth with Lexol leather cleaner and rubbed it over Whisper's saddle, taking extra care to clean the stirrup leathers which always trapped dirt.

I did the same to her bridle and tossed the towel in the bin for dirty saddle pads, cloths, and blankets. Now

Whisper's tack had a subtle sheen—much better. I took a stark white saddle pad from my pile and put all of her tack over my arm.

When I reached her stall, I put down the tack and peered over the stall door. Whisper was sound asleep in the back corner of her stall. *Très* adorable! Her head was down and her eyes closed. A hind leg was cocked and she blew out gentle breaths that sounded like tiny snores.

"Hi, baby girl," I whispered, not wanting to startle her. "I'm so happy to see you!"

Whisper flicked an ear toward my voice and blinked. I opened the stall door and walked up to her. I loved watching her curly eyelashes flutter.

"You're so cute. You made me feel so much less nervous about testing today and all you had to do was be yourself. We're riding for Mr. Conner to see which team we should be on. I *really* want to make the intermediate team, but not if Mr. Conner doesn't think we're ready. We should be on the right team for *us*. If it's the beginner team—okay."

I'd thought about it some last night. I was once a nationally ranked dressage champion. I'd even ridden at some of the best stables in the entire country.

But my accident had changed a lot.

It hadn't changed my abilities as a rider—it had affected my confidence. Building back confidence was something I worked on every single day.

"Let's get you groomed and tacked up, missy," I said to Whisper. "We're going to make you extra pretty today."

Whisper seemed to understand the P-word. I stepped half out of the stall and took her baby blue halter off the rack. I buckled it over her head and led her out of the stall. Our usual pair of crossties was free. Within moments, Whisper's beauty treatment was under way.

"I never told you this," I said to her. "But when I was looking for a horse, I secretly hoped I'd find a mare." I swept the body brush across Whisper's back. "You look *très belle* in candy pink and pale blue—my favorite colors. Ordering gifts for you this summer was so fun."

Brielle, Ana, and I had spent hours online ordering glittery bell boots; a pale blue water bucket; pink, violet, blue, and yellow saddle pads; and soft cotton halters in a rainbow of colors.

It took minutes to make Whisper's gray coat shine. Her mane and tail were next, then I picked out her hooves. I ran the hoof pick along the edges of each shoe checking for any tiny pebbles I might have missed—all clear.

I opened my tack trunk and pulled out hoof polish. "Polish time!"

Crouching down, I applied generous coats of shiny black polish to all of her hooves. They'd have plenty of time to dry before we hit the arena. For fun, I often painted her hooves with glittery polish. But today was a glitter-free zone.

When I'd been on the show circuit, I had a routine before my class. I told my horse about my fears so they were out of my head, spent extra time warming up, and when I entered the arena, I imagined Taylor, Becs, Brielle, Ana, and my parents in the stands ready to cheer me on.

I picked up Whisper's saddle pad, running my hand over it to smooth out any wrinkles. Her ears flicked lazily back and forth, her hind leg cocked.

"Looks like one of us isn't worried," I teased. "I want to be cool like you. Not put so much pressure on this. No matter what class we're in, we'll still be training. From everything Kim told me about Mr. Conner, he won't put us on a team if he's not a hundred percent sure that we're both ready. Maybe we need to start on the beginner team so that we can grow best together as a team—I don't know."

Both of Whisper's ears swiveled back as she listened. I

patted her shoulder before picking up the saddle. Hoisting it into the air, I placed it gently on her back and positioned it just right.

"Everything changes today, Wisp," I told her softly, tightening the girth. "Everything."

I picked up her bridle and unhooked the crossties. Suddenly, something wonderful occurred to me. "I've never shown on my *own* horse, Wisp! Can you imagine?! I can't even imagine hearing the announcer say it! 'Lauren Towers riding *her horse*—Whisper.' I've only ever heard my name called along with a stable horse."

Holding on to Whisper's reins, I put her tack box on top of the trunk, shut the stall door, and made sure I hadn't left anything out in the aisle. I checked my clothes to make sure I was ready.

Shirt: clean.

Breeches: spotless.

Boots: shiny.

Grin: ear to ear.

I put on my velvet show helmet. I intended for Mr. Conner to see that I was taking today seriously.

"Ready, pretty?" I asked. "We have . . ." I checked my watch. "Plenty of time to warm up and then head to the big arena."

I picked up my BlackBerry to type a quick text to Becca. I was sure she hadn't forgotten about my test, but I wanted to be sure she was sending big-sister-good-luck vibes at four-forty on the dot.

My phone blinked. BBMs.

Becca: Lauren, you are going to KILL it. I have no doubt. I'm awesome and we share the same DNA so . . .

I laughed and kept reading.

BBM the sec ur done & tell me abt it. Kiss Whisper 4 me. Love u both! xx

Taylor: I know ur testing today. GL, LT! You'll b perfect!

Brielle: You don't need luck 4 2day! BBM or Skype me later!

Ana: Don't b nervous. Ur going 2 b amazing. ☺

I locked my phone and put it in my trunk. I knew I wouldn't need to message Becs. Not only had she remembered—every single one of my friends had remembered about today.

Wow.

Just because I wasn't in Union didn't mean they'd forgotten about me. I smiled, feeling their warmth all the way in Canterwood.

I led Whisper down the aisle.

We passed the big indoor arena where a girl in my history class trotted a blue roan in circles.

Mr. Conner, broad arms crossed, watched and wrote on the paper held in place by an obviously well-worn clipboard.

Keep walking. It'll only make you nervous if you stay in one place.

Turning Whisper away, I walked her to the other arena. Six or seven other riders warmed up inside. I recognized two—Kacie Freeman and Jayllex Mason—from some of my classes. Khloe had told me that they were trying out for intermediate. And she'd been honest when I'd asked. She'd said they were both good riders.

I settled into Whisper's saddle and pretended I had blinders on. I didn't allow myself to watch anyone else.

Whisper walked on a loose rein to the arena wall. I made sure the positions I'd learned from day one of riding were correct: toes up, heels down, a light hold on the reins, knees bent at the right angle, back straight but not too much, and elbows tucked in.

Someone stood in the doorway, a bright orange shirt that caught my eye.

I glanced over. Riley stood in the entrance, leaning against the wall. She waved, giving me a huge smile.

I didn't know what she wanted, but I knew one thing: I was not going to let her throw off my practice.

Whisper eyed the other horses, craning her neck to look. I squeezed my legs against her sides and did a half halt to get her attention back where it belonged: on me. I made sure I did the same in return and made sure not to look at Riley.

I asked Whisper for a trot and her gait was smooth as could be—the transition seamless. Her hooves barely made a sound in the arena dirt.

I took her through easy exercises during our warm-up—nothing that would exhaust her. And, though I didn't look at Riley once, I felt her there, still in the doorway.

I eased Whisper from a trot to a walk. "Good job, girl," I said. I leaned forward and patted her neck. "You did great."

I checked my watch. Time to head over to the arena. Whisper and I could go inside in a few minutes. Dismounting, I eased the reins over Whisper's head and headed for the exit.

Riley, her long hair in a high ponytail, walked up to us.

Treat her like any other competitor, I told myself. *She can pull the mean girl act all she wants, but I will be professional.*

"Lauren, wow," Riley said, smiling. But her smile wasn't warm—it was subzero.

"Thanks," I kept walking. "We have to get to the arena."

Riley caught up and walked beside me. "I'm sure you'll do the best you can with all of the pressure. We're all so lucky to be here and riding for Mr. Conner. He's one of the best instructors in the country."

"True. We're all very lucky," I said, walking a bit faster.

"A lot of riders are intimidated by him," she persisted. "I can tell that you're not. I don't know how you're so calm. I thought about everything testing meant and how it would affect my entire year. It scared me that this was the *one* chance I had to determine what team I'd ride for until I could test again next spring."

"I'm not focused on what *team* I'll make," I said. "I'm riding for Mr. Conner. That's it. Whatever decision he makes is mine to respect."

"Just as well. The beginner team sounds like a better fit for you," Riley said. "Less pressure, new student, you know the drill."

She was trying so hard to shake me, it was almost humorous now.

We reached the big arena. There were still five minutes before I could go in. The horse and rider I'd seen before were gone now. Mr. Conner shifted through some papers on a long wooden table along the wall.

"Riley," I said. "Your pep talk was exactly what I needed

to hear." I kept a smile on my face and sarcasm out of my voice. "As Madame LaFleur would want us to say, *'Merci!'*"

"De rien," Riley said, her tone not so cheery. "Got to go!"

When she was gone, I buried my face in Whisper's neck, giggling.

"That was way too funny," I said. "Maybe she'll think twice before trying to mess with us again."

I took a slow breath in. It had taken so much to get to this point. Gratefulness for so many things overwhelmed me.

My dream horse. The opportunity to ride for Mr. Conner. My acceptance to Canterwood. New friends. Old friends. A family that supported me.

No matter what team I made, I was proud to say I was a student and equestrian at Canterwood Crest Academy.

"Let's do this, girl."

I mounted, and Whisper stood still as I lowered myself into the saddle. I didn't wait another second. I squeezed my legs against her sides, and she walked through the entrance. This arena was *huge*. It had room to jump, practice dressage, and do group work with many other riders.

The vaulted ceiling's wooden beams were light and polished-looking. On the far side large windows let

sunshine inside. At the front of the arena, an empty sky-box looked like prime real estate. I wondered if we were allowed to watch the advanced team or even the YENT practice. If I *ever* got to watch Sasha Silver ride . . .

Mr. Conner walked to the exit door and handed a sheet of paper to the groom named Doug. Doug, tan and lanky, took the paper and left. Mr. Conner looked every bit the serious, high-level instructor. His dark hair was cropped short. He was tall and muscular, and he had an obvious tan from constantly working outside with the horses. I couldn't imagine him putting up with much from girls like Riley.

He smiled and walked over. "Hello, Lauren," he said. He extended a hand to me, his brown eyes warm.

I shook his hand. My tiny hand worked to hold its own in his sincere and very firm welcoming grip. "It's nice to meet you, Mr. Conner," I said, the strength in my voice surprising me.

My heart pounded so hard it hurt. This was it. He would judge me before I even got to ride.

"Lauren," Mr. Conner's voice was gentle, "today you're entering my arena as a brand-new rider. I want to be honest—I've watched you compete and am aware of your past titles in dressage. You're young, but you've already made huge strides in the equestrian world."

"Thank you," I said, still unsure where this conversation would take us.

"But none of that will be considered today," Mr. Conner said.

I still wasn't sure if this was good news or bad. I nodded, despite my confusion.

He seemed to sense my confusion because, after a short pause, he continued. "No performance but this one will count when you test," Mr. Conner clarified. "A few rules have changed recently, so I want to be sure everything about this test ride will be clear. So please, feel free to ask me questions at any point." He put his clipboard in his other hand. "Sound good?" he asked me, smiling.

"Yes, sir," I said. "Thank you."

He nodded and continued with what sounded like a much-practiced speech. "A student must remain on a team for an entire school year before he or she may test for a higher level. Tests are held each fall and the following spring. Spring is a chance for students to begin on a new team the coming fall."

I nodded.

"No incoming students are placed on the advanced team no matter what his or her background," Mr. Conner continued. "The riding program has added several new instructors to teach various classes. We are not solely focused on showing. Instead, the goal is to build a strong team of horse and rider. Each grade will have to complete a course centered on horse care and equine knowledge. This is a new component required of this semester."

I loved this—riding wasn't just for me. I wanted Whisper healthy, too.

"Each student will be quizzed periodically on materials covered," Mr. Conner added. He reached out and stroked Whisper's neck. She swished her tail, content. "I understand that you and Whisper are relatively new partners."

I nodded, beaming. "She's the first horse I've ever owned. I searched a long time to find her, but I'm so glad I did."

Mr. Conner looked at us both as if searching to see if he felt our bond.

"I knew right away when I saw her."

Mr. Conner smiled, nodding silently. As quickly as that faraway looked appeared in his face, it was gone and we were back to business. "I'd be remiss not to speak more with you about your history before the test, as your case is a special one. As I expect you've been told, I've spoken with Kim and your parents." I nodded for him to continue. "I do not want you to feel that you're going

to be pressured to begin competing before you're ready."

"Thank you," I said. "I appreciate that very much. Kim did tell me that it wasn't something I had to worry about. One the other hand, I do want you to know that I came here because I have hope of showing again—when you think I'm ready."

"Excellent, Lauren. I'm glad to know what your thoughts are about going forward," he said. "*No one* will be showing for a while, and riders, unless they are on the Youth Equestrian National Team, are allowed to decide their own show schedule."

"Do I have to decide today?" I asked.

"No," Mr. Conner said. "The only thing you have to do today is go through a few exercises while I take notes."

I nodded. "Okay!" I looked down at my horse. *My horse!* Would I ever get used to saying that? "I'm ready when you are."

22

FEAR MONSTERS AND LURKING LOSERS

"ALL RIGHT. NOW, I'D LIKE FOR YOU TO follow some commands as I give them. Know I'm not *judging* you," Mr. Conner said. "I'm merely deciding where you skills fit in among the other Canterwood riders in your grade. So . . . let's get started!"

I nodded. I'd showed hundreds of times, but this test really mattered to me.

"Please take Whisper along the wall, clockwise, and trot," Mr. Conner said.

I turned Whisper away from him and asked her to trot. I posted while we kept an even distance away from the wall as we made our way around the arena.

"Sitting trot," Mr. Conner commanded.

I sat deep in the saddle. We passed the large window

facing the outdoor arena and, out of the corner of my eye, I saw a flash of brilliant red hair as a girl on a chestnut took a jump. Whisper strained against the reins to look out the window, both ears pointed forward. I tapped my heels against her sides and urged her forward. *You threw Whisper off,* I told myself.

We lapped the arena again and, this time, Whisper didn't even try to glance outside.

"Reverse directions and canter," Mr. Conner called.

I turned Whisper toward the center of the arena, making a half loop, and realigned her along the wall as we trotted in the opposite direction. I shifted my weight in the saddle, gave her more rein, and squeezed my legs. Whisper's bloodlines made her canter smooth.

"Canter another half a lap," Mr. Conner called. "Then cross the center and do a flying lead change." He walked out of the center to give us space.

Flying lead changes were one of my favorite things to do on horseback. There was a rush when, for a fraction of a second, all four of the horse's legs were midair. A thousand-plus-pound horse and I were airborne because of a command *I* gave.

Whisper's hooves pounded the arena surface rhythmically. Her canter needed to stay strong and collected.

We reached the halfway point of the arena, and, gently, I pulled the rein guiding her to the center. I made sure she kept up momentum as we neared the arena's center. I kept my inside leg against the girth and my outside leg just behind it.

When we hit the middle of the arena, I swapped the positions of my legs. My hands stayed soft to give Whisper enough room to stretch her body—especially her neck. Whisper, responding to my leg aids, bent through her entire body, and we suspended in the air. She struck out with the opposite leg, completing the move. I kept her canter controlled as we moved on the new lead.

Mr. Conner walked back to the center of the arena. "Slow to a trot and a walk, then come to the center," he directed.

Within strides, we were at a walk and halting in front of Mr. Conner. I patted Whisper's shoulder. I couldn't have asked her for more. She was doing amazingly—it felt as though we were especially in sync today, like we'd been a team for years rather than a mere couple of months.

"Really great job, Lauren," Mr. Conner said.

"Thank you, sir," I said. I tried not to look the way I felt: happy, joyful, moved to tears, and more than anything, validated. Mr. Conner was not known for doling

out compliment after compliment. Nor was he known for going easy on his students. When he paid you a compliment, it *meant* something.

Whisper's ears pointed to Mr. Conner. The mare recognized praise. I ran my hand along her neck. She wasn't even a bit sweaty or out of breath.

"Take a few moments to regroup while Mike and I set up dressage markers," Mr. Conner said. "I'll call out instructions for a simple test. Then we'll go to the outdoor jump course."

Jump course. My mouth felt full of sawdust. I'd been jumping at Kim's all summer. She'd even worked extensively with me on cross-country and stadium jumping. But there was more than a tiny lingering fear that hadn't gone away. The Monster of Fear inside me had dissipated with each jump I conquered. Still, in stressful situations the monster fear was strong. Sometimes stronger than I.

Mr. Conner walked out of the arena, returning seconds later with Mike. I kicked my feet out of the stirrups and let Whisper amble at a walk on a loose rein.

Old Lauren, the one with national dressage titles, wouldn't have blinked at the thought of jumping. She would have been excited and ready to tackle any obstacle Mr. Conner would dare put in her way.

New Lauren, though, had invisible scars. Scars that fed the monster and made every jump terrifying—even though it had been almost two years since the New Lauren was born.

Focus on one thing at a time, I told myself. Dressage was my first love. This was my chance to show Mr. Conner my passion.

Mike and Mr. Conner put down the last white marker. Finally, Mike, who gave me a thumbs-up, left the arena. Mr. Conner walked to the arena entrance and stopped. "Please ride to the entrance, and I'll give you commands from there."

I walked Whisper to the entrance. Something moved in the skybox. I looked up, and Riley, peering through the glass, waved at me. Did she not understand the meaning of a *closed* test? But maybe she knew me better than I thought—because no way would I tell Mr. Conner that some gossipy spoiled brat with way too much free time had come to sabotage my placement test.

Riley would never mean more to me than my ride.

I focused on turning Whisper to face Mr. Conner and the markers. I straightened my shoulders and never looked Riley's way again. I'd ridden in front of hundreds of people. And if Whisper and I could perform for Mr. Conner, we could take on one skybox-lurking loser.

"I'll be looking for a few things during your ride," Mr. Conner said, looking up at me. "Suppleness, regularity of gaits, balance, activity in the transitions, and lightness of aids, among other things. Please begin at a working trot and halt at *X*."

We trotted into the arena, stopped, and I saluted.

"Track right to *C* at a working trot," Mr. Conner said. "At *B*, circle right fifteen diameters."

Whisper moved with ease to *C* and completed an even circle at *B*.

"Working canter from *B* to *K*, then trot to *E*," Mr. Conner said.

Whisper was on her game. And so was I. Riley and my Monster of Fear had vanished.

Whisper's movements were active. She made a balanced transition to a working canter. She slowed the moment I asked for a trot, and her hindquarters remained engaged.

"Complete a ten-diameter circle at *E* and free walk to *M*," Mr. Conner called out.

Whisper's balance was a touch off when we started our circle at *E*, but she collected herself. When we completed the circle, I slowed her to a walk, giving her lots of rein to stretch.

"Return to *X* at a trot and halt," Mr. Conner said.

Going back to X meant we were finished. I asked Whisper for a trot, and she took an extra stride at a walk before she listened to my cue to trot. Strides before X, I prepared myself to bring her to a halt on the mark. Just before X, I closed my fingers around the reins while releasing the pressure on her sides. Whisper stopped and didn't move—not even a swish of her tail—while I saluted. Relief surged through me. Two parts of the test down!

"Thank you, Lauren," Mr. Conner said. "Please follow me to the outdoor arena."

He opened a large side door, and I rode Whisper through after him. At the arena entrance, a taped-up sign read: CLOSED FOR TESTING. Inside, two verticals, an oxer, a double oxer, a higher vertical, and a double combination awaited us.

No riders were near this arena. I didn't expect Riley to follow me outside. The arena was too open, and Mr. Conner would send her away for sure.

"There are six jumps that you'll take in order," Mr. Conner said. "It's pretty straightforward." I nodded as he explained the course to me. Then he stepped away for me to start.

My heartbeat sounded as loud to me as Whisper's hooves when she cantered. No way had I come this far to

choke. Whatever I thought about Laurens Old and New was gone. All I knew was this: Lauren always gave it a shot.

"Begin when you're ready," Mr. Conner said. "And remember—don't rush, and trust your horse."

I didn't give myself a second more to think. I led Whisper into a trot, then a canter. Her rhythmic strides got us to the first jump in seconds. I lifted out of the saddle and pushed my hands a few inches up along her neck. We cleared the red-and-white-striped rails. My head was up—gaze on the next jump. Wind *whooshed* in my ears. One jump down.

Whisper's canter remained collected as we reached the second vertical. The three-foot-high jump had rails that resembled wood. Whisper didn't blink. She tucked her forelegs under her and propelled off the ground. Whisper snorted, tossing her head as we landed. I couldn't help but smile—seeing Whisper have fun made me feel happy and more confident.

Whisper took the oxer without pause and we made a half circle to change directions. Whisper's body stretched over the double oxer, clearing the spread. We cantered toward the vertical—the highest—and scariest jump of the course.

It wouldn't help Whisper if she sensed my nerves. Six strides later, I rose out of the saddle again and gave Whisper rein. I knew I'd made a mistake. Whisper took off a millisecond too late. Her knees knocked the top rail. Whisper's ears flicked back in displeasure.

I squeezed my knees against her, urging her toward the double combo. The tricky part was timing. Something I did *not* feel confident about after our last jump. But I had to shake this one mistake or we'd *definitely* make more. Whisper could only take one stride between the jumps. I slowed Whisper just before the rails, and this time we were in the air at the perfect time.

She landed clean on the other side and took one stride, and then I asked her to jump again. Whisper collected herself and thrust her gray body into the air, clearing the other half of the combo.

I didn't know whether to smile or cry. I couldn't have been more proud of Whisper—she hadn't faltered once. I felt like we'd done our best, even if our best had meant a knocked rail. Would the pole on the ground take away any chance at the intermediate team? Mr. Conner's face gave away nothing. Our fate was out of my hands and into his.

"Nice work, Lauren," he said. "Thank you for allowing

me to evaluate your riding. I'll review my notes tonight. Come to my office after school tomorrow and we'll discuss my decision. Then you'll join your team for a lesson."

"Thank you, Mr. Conner," I said. "For everything."

23

FINALLY FINDING . . .

WHISPER

AT THE END OF THE DAY I WAS AT MY DESK making my way through the pile of first-day homework. Khloe paged through her history textbook in front of her own desk.

Testing had been much earlier, but my brain felt as though I'd finished minutes ago. As promised, Khloe had been waiting by Whisper's stall after I'd cooled down. She clasped her hands together, bouncing on her toes, when I told her an edited version (i.e., no talk of Old Lauren) of my test. Khloe seemed so sure I'd make the intermediate team, but I truly had no idea where I'd wind up.

Khloe swiveled her desk chair to face me. "What do you have left?" she asked, lifting her leg and pointing a toe at my carefully organized assignments.

"Just that paper for English," I said.

"I don't know how you did it," Khloe said.

I took a sip of tea—green with pomegranate. "Did what?" I asked.

"All of that homework so fast after testing." Khloe spun her desk chair in a lazy circle. "I couldn't focus on *anything* the night after I tested. It took me until three or four in the morning to get everything done. I had the attention span of a fruit fly."

"It's easy for me to lose myself in homework," I said. "The assignments weren't as bad as I thought, but there were a lot. I always feel better staying busy. If I have nothing to do, I'll just obsess about testing."

"Understood," Khloe said. "After we finish, want to grab a late dinner in the caf?"

"Sounds great. Hopefully, we'll be going at a weird enough time that Riley won't be there."

Khloe made a gagging-slash-grumbling sound in her throat. "*Don't* even say her name to me. I can't believe she was in the skybox during your test. Well, I take that back. I *do* believe it. That gross little . . ."

I knew what was coming.

"Lurker!"

I'd shared my own nicker for Riley the Reiler, and ever

since, Khloe had been trying it out in different ways every ten to fifteen minutes.

"I know she was trying to make me nervous," I said. "And it worked, but only for, like, a second."

"I bet she's worried now after she saw you ride. She's lucky you're more mature than she is. If you'd told Mr. Conner what she did, she'd be in huge trouble."

"She's not even worth it, Khlo," I said. "For now I'll even refrain from immature nicknames until she does something nuts."

Khloe pouted. "Nooo—*more* nicknames! You're good at them!"

I laughed at her pitiful expression and we went back to our computers.

Homework had definitely kept my mind off testing. After I'd completed each assignment, I'd put it in the pale pink TURN IN folder in my binder. Each assignment got checked off when I finished. There was only one left with no check mark—*write English paper.*

I stared at the blank Word document. The cursor blinked, taunting me. Mr. Davidson had asked us to write three to five pages about ourselves—something we wanted him to know about us. I'd been brainstorming while making cup after cup of tea and hadn't come up with a single

interesting idea. Writing the "I have two sisters, live in Union, love horses" seemed generic-slash-boring. It felt like a "what I did this summer" essay.

What do I want him to know about me? What makes me Lauren Towers? Why am I at Canterwood?

An idea rushed into my brain. No way. No. I was not writing about *that*. I'd just write about moving or something. There was no way I was ready to write that story. I couldn't.

My palms sweated. No one else was going to see this paper. Thinking about it—my accident—was something I'd been avoiding since I'd arrived on campus. At least, I thought I'd been avoiding it, but it never went away. The always-looming secret had been there when I'd met Khloe, had a tea party in the common room, and gone on a trail ride with Lexa.

If I took this chance to write it, it could bring me one step closer to being able to tell my new friends. Lexa and Khloe deserved to know the real me, and they wouldn't until I shared my past with them. I still wasn't ready to *talk* about it, but could I be ready to write about it?

I typed my name, the date, and the class on the page. I hadn't even started to type the title when the memories of that day began to assault me, to flood me and force me to go back to that cold November day.

I'd been competing at the Red Oak Horse Trial in Washington, D.C. I was points away from being overall champion and clinching a win for my stable, Double Aces. All year I'd shown every chance I had. I rode even when I shouldn't have—hiding the flu from my parents and instructor, pushing through a nasty cold, and competing with a bruised shoulder from a fall during practice.

My mount, Skyblue, was one of the best stable horses I'd ever ridden. We had a tight bond and I adored him. The dapple gray gelding never questioned any of my commands, and he worked hard to please me.

At Red Oak it had been our turn for cross-country. We'd blasted out of the starting box at a gallop and had covered the course fast. I'd known how good our time was and that we could take it easy over the final jumps, but Skyblue wasn't tired and adrenaline pumped through me. I'd kept him moving as fast as possible, barely slowing when necessary, and we raced toward the final vertical before the finish line.

The crowd cheered when they saw us, and it added to my excitement. I started counting strides—ready to lift out of the saddle for the jump—but I never got the chance. Without warning, Skyblue had slammed to a halt. I remember feeling confused that I was flying through the air without my horse.

My body crashed into the cold, hard ground. Screams filled my ears, and my eyes fluttered open to see Mom and Dad bent over me, expressions on their faces I'd never seen before. Mom's skin was gray. I tried to open my mouth to ask what was wrong, but I couldn't.

Darkness swallowed me. I woke up later, in the hospital, with machines beeping in my ears and an IV in my arm.

I pulled myself out of the memory and looked down. My hands had balled into fists. I uncurled them, flexing my fingers. My nails had left half-moon shapes on my palms.

I'd remembered having been in and out as paramedics eased me onto a stretcher and into an ambulance. I asked about Skyblue—worried that he'd been hurt. My old instructor, Mr. Wells, told me Skyblue was fine. I spent a night in the hospital and was released the next day with permission to ride when my soreness went away.

Skyblue and I had escaped without any serious injuries, but I'd been hurt in a way I couldn't understand. That had been my first serious fall. I never found out what happened. I didn't know why Skyblue had halted—if I'd done something to cause it or if he'd been spooked. Regardless, I couldn't stop blaming myself for putting Skyblue

in jeopardy. Mom and Dad, figuring I was resilient and as eager as ever to ride, had offered to take me to the stable a few days after my fall. I experienced a feeling then that I'd never felt around horses before: fear.

After that I became a master of excuses. I made up excuse after excuse about why I couldn't ride.

I never rode Skyblue again.

I took a long break from riding, period, before finally deciding to try again when we moved to Union. Kim knew all about my past, and she'd been the one to help me learn to manage my fear and finally even jump again.

I'd never be *that* Lauren again—the Lauren who forgot what was important and pushed herself and her horse unnecessarily. I learned how to have a life with horses *and* friends—something I didn't have when I was showing so often. Ana and Brielle had gotten me involved at school, and I realized how much I liked having something other than riding in my life.

I started typing and the words spilled onto the pages. Everything from that day—from the confidence I'd had, the exhilaration of what seemed like a sure win, the sensation of flying through the air and crashing into the ground, the screams of the crowd, the blurry faces, and the smell of alcohol and the prick of the needle when a

nurse gave me an IV—went onto the page. Seven pages later, I was done. I saved the document. It felt as if I'd just purged a big part of the secret that had been haunting me for so long.

"You were *really* into your essay," Khloe said. "It must be good!" I noticed that all her books were packed and her desk was clear. "What's it about?"

I turned back to close my laptop, trying to think of what to say. I was the worst liar!

"It's about . . ." I paused. "Looking for the right horse and finally finding Whisper."

"Aw, that's great," Khloe said. "You're so passionate— I'm sure you'll get an A."

"Thanks." I smiled, but didn't feel happy. This was the worst way to start a friendship. Maybe there wouldn't even be a friendship if she ever found out that I'd just lied to her.

"I'm going to shower," Khloe said. "Then do you want to grab dinner?"

"Sounds great."

While Khloe showered, I printed my essay, put it in my homework file, and shoved it deep into my bag.

24

MY REASON
TO LIVE!

I THOUGHT YESTERDAY HAD GONE BY FAST? Not even *close* to today. Math and history had been a blur—both of my teachers had acted as if school had been in session for weeks. Mr. Spellman had told us to take notes—all of which he'd collect at the end of every week that he would then grade and count toward our participation grade.

I'd always taken detailed notes, but he talked *so* fast, I'd had to scribble and abbreviate most of my sentences— sometimes in French! My handwriting was illegible in some places. I'd have to recopy the notes tonight.

In English, I'd kept my essay tucked away in my homework folder until the last possible second. Khloe sat next to me, with Clare beside her, and I only took out my paper when Mr. Davidson started collecting them. When the papers left my hands, it felt as though something I'd watched over and kept quiet about and protected from everything real in the world had snuck out in the middle of the night and now was gone.

By the time I got to lunch, my arms were full of books and papers. I hadn't even had time to put everything away into my bag.

"Tomato soup and oyster crackers, please," I said to the lunch lady. She filled a big bowl with steaming soup and gave me a few packets of crackers. I picked up the tray, barely able to hold it and my school stuff. I shifted my books, trying to rest them on my hip and my tray jiggled, soup sloshing over the bowl's side.

"Need some help?" I heard someone ask.

I looked up from my tray and stared into a sea of stormy deep blue eyes.

"I'm Drew," the guy said. "I can take your tray . . . unless you were trying to paint your white sweater with red balloons?"

"I want to laugh," I said. "But if I do, I'm afraid I'll drop something. So yes. And thank you."

Drew took my tray and I readjusted my books—some in my bag, with two left to carry. "I'm Lauren Towers," I said.

Drew smiled, showing off straight white teeth. His skin, as pale as my own, made his black hair look even darker.

"So I can't help but noticed you still have one bag and two books. So, I mean, I sort of have to carry your soup to your table. Unless"—he gestured to the lunch tray—"you want to risk it?"

"That seems . . . unnecessarily risky." I laughed.

We left the lunch line and stepped into the caf together.

"You're new, right?" Drew asked. "I think I've seen you around the stable."

"I am new," I said. "*And* I'm a rider, so you probably *have* seen me at the stable."

"Did you try out for a riding team?" Drew asked. "I'm an intermediate rider."

"I did—yesterday. And intermediate is just what I'm hoping to be. I find out this afternoon."

I'd been so into our conversation that I hadn't even realized we'd been ambling through the caf. I looked over, and Khloe and Lexa, sitting where we'd been yesterday, were staring with wide eyes and grins on their faces.

"I'm sitting over there," I said, tilting my head in their direction. Drew followed me to my table.

Once there, he put my tray next to Khloe's.

"Hey, guys," he said to them.

"Hey," both girls said. They stared at me. Then at Drew. Then me. Then Drew. Back and forth. I shot them a *Stop it!* glare.

"Thank you so much for helping me," I sad.

"Oh, well, you know—I *had* to. I mean, I know how much you hate red balloons."

I laughed. "Well, my white sweater thanks you."

"See you around, Lauren," Drew said. "I hope you make the intermediate team."

"Thanks, Drew. I hope so, too."

I slid into my seat, staring after him as he walked away.

My eyes stopped on a face as red as my tomato soup. Riley, seated a few tables away with Clare, stared daggers at me. I looked away, shaking my head.

"Riley looks as if she wants to kill me," I said to Lexa and Khloe. "What's her problem?"

The girls looked at each other, then at me.

"Oh, I don't know," Khloe said. "Maybe because you're a boy magnet!"

Lexa nodded, her curls bouncing. "That's Riley's 'thing.' Riley always got attention from all the guys in our grade."

"Not anymore," Khloe singsonged, pointing at me.

"You're both crazy," I said. I ripped open a packet of crackers and put them into my soup. "I almost dropped my tray of soup and Drew happened to be there. He doesn't *like* me—he was just being polite."

"Let's do a count, shall we?" Khloe asked. "Monday: Zack. Garret. Tuesday: Drew. Three guys in two days have talked to you and all of them have made the *I'm going to ask you out soon* face."

I swallowed a sip of soup. "You're ridiculous. I'm not interested in going out with anyone right now. Okay, three boys talked to me. It was like that at all my old schools. I always talked to the boys as much as I spoke to the girls. I just feel comfortable around them."

"I so wish I were you," Lexa said. She brushed a French bread crumb from her silver satin three-quarters-sleeve shirt. "Whenever I try to even talk to a boy, I get all sweaty and mess up everything I want to say. It's so embarrassing."

"The more you talk to boys," I said, "the more you realize there's nothing to be nervous about. I think they're actually more scared to talk to you."

"And by 'you,'" Khloe said, "you mean *us?*"

"No—I mean *most* girls, but especially girly ones," I said.

"You're supergirly!" Lexa said. "You *scream* girly!"

"Yes," I said, pointing an oyster cracker at her. "But I'm also into sports and camping and dares . . . and other such boy-type things."

"Why do we have to change for them, though?" Khloe asked. "I mean, a guy could get to know me by watching *Sin City Celebrities* with me."

Khloe and Lex both tilted their heads at me.

"True," I said. "But they're the ones who ask us out. It's probably a lot of pressure. They have to worry about us saying yes or no."

"Huh," Lexa said finally. "So if they do girly things with us, that's still scary."

"I never thought about it like that," Khloe said. "We *should* make them nervous!"

We laughed and ate the rest of our lunch. I fielded more questions about boys. The easy chatter kept me laughing—*and* from obsessing about the results of yesterday's testing.

Riding was *far* from my brain when I walked up to the art building for my first fashion class. The glass-and-steel building stood out among all of Canterwood's other brick structures. My black flats were silent on the swirls of the gray-and-white-marble floor.

This felt like a dream. I always thought I'd have to wait until college to study fashion! When I reached my classroom and peered inside, other students were chatting in groups.

In one corner, mannequins stood as if beckoning to be draped in beautiful fabric.

I posted a fast Chatter update: *LaurBell: The fashion bldg—c'est mon raison d être!*

I couldn't believe Ms. Utz, the math teacher-slash-guidance-counselor, almost hadn't let me take this course. She'd been concerned that I was taking on too many activities. But once I sent her an impassioned e-mail explaining my love of fashion and that I thrived on a heavy workload, she'd allowed it. Besides, fashion didn't even count as a class—it would be fun!

I took a seat near the front row and plucked a new notebook—a yellow one with a sketch of a cocktail dress—from my bag, along with my textbook and a pencil.

"Lauren?"

"Oh, hey," I said, looking up. "Cole?"

I hadn't noticed before, but Cole was a fab dresser. Today his attire was casual-slash-dressy: A hunter-green Ralph Lauren polo (bonus points for the large logo). Jeans: vintage-washed whiskered slim fit. Shoes: black leather *Ferragamos*?!

"Cool if I sit by you?" he asked.

"Of course." I gestured to the seat next to mine.

He slipped his messenger bag over the back of his chair and sat down. As he looked around his green eyes were probably as wide as mine had been seconds ago.

"Fashion at Canterwood," Cole said. "It's like they tried to make a course for me."

I laughed. "Really? I feel the same way. Too bad it's only twice a week."

"No kidding," Cole said. He smoothed his shirt and ran a hand through his light brown hair.

I couldn't help but stare at his shoes. When I realized drool was practically coming out of my mouth, I saw he was laughing.

"Sorry, but are those . . ."

"Custom-made black Italian leather—"

"Ferragamos!" We said in unison.

"*Never* go shopping without me," I said.

"Deal," he promised, laughing.

A woman walked into the room and stood in front of the desk. She looked as if she'd just stepped out of *Vogue*. She'd paired a white ruffled V-neck shirt with a black skirt and ankle boots. Her dark brown hair, with caramel-colored highlights, was flatironed and hung just below her shoulders.

"Hello, class," she said. "I'm Ms. Snow, your teacher for this class."

Beside me, Cole straightened. I was so happy to have a fashion soul mate at Canterwood.

"Today's going to be very brief." Ms. Snow smiled. "I don't believe in overloading my students right away. You're free to use the end of the period to read or do homework."

Oui! Even though I already loved this class, I had so much work to do that I was grateful.

Ms. Snow handed a syllabus to all of us and went through each point. Required reading covered fashion through the ages, fashion icon biographies from past to present, designers and their most famous creations, and exciting other topics! Not even one sounded boring.

"Along with the reading," Ms. Snow said, "we'll also have a big project due each semester. The first assignment will require a partner of your choice."

Cole and I looked at each other at the same time, grinning. "Yay!" he mouthed.

"I know!" I mouthed back.

"Let's do quick introductions," Ms. Snow said. She pointed to the first desk on the left.

"I'm Raquel, and I picked fashion because I love to sketch clothes," she said.

Ms. Snow gestured to me.

"Hi, I'm Lauren," I said. "I've read about style icons and the history of fashion since I was little, and this class was the first one I picked from the catalog."

"Great," Ms. Snow said. After a few more people, Ms. Snow reached Cole.

"I'm Cole. I chose fashion because I want to be a designer someday," he said.

Wow—I was impressed!

We were going to make a fabulous team—especially since Cole said he'd been sketching for years. He'd be able to teach me *a lot.*

When we'd finished, Ms. Snow smiled. "I want to take a moment to tell you why I'm teaching this course. It won't be too long and boring, I promise. I'll open the floor to questions before allowing you to study or do your homework."

Ms. Snow walked to her desk, perching on the edge and tucking her hair behind her ear. "I was a total tomboy growing up," she said. "I didn't know anything about fashion, nor did I ever want to. I thought wearing my brother's oversized sweatshirt and jeans with holes in the knees was 'in.'" We all laughed with her.

"I didn't develop an interest in fashion through middle

school or high school like you. But in college, I was an art history major. In one of my classes, we covered a few chapters about the evolution of clothes through history. We had to write an essay about our favorite piece of clothing from the times we'd studied and discuss how it was 'art.'"

Ms. Snow looked at us. "You know what I did?"

We shook our heads.

"I didn't write the paper."

Cole and I turned to each other, trading surprised glances. I'd *never* had a teacher like Ms. Snow. She was so honest and relatable.

"Did you fail the class?" a girl asked.

"Yeah, did you have to make up the paper?" questioned someone else.

Ms. Snow smiled and walked to the center of the room.

"My professor called me to his office and asked why I'd missed the assignment," she said. "I'd always turned in every piece of homework and he didn't understand why I hadn't asked for an extension or talked to him about it. I told him I didn't see fashion as art and asked if I could write something—*anything*—else."

I rested my hand on my chin, curious.

"Of course he said *no*. And in addition, he told me my paper had to be five pages longer. He reminded me the

paper was worth twenty percent of my grade and was not something I wanted to fail."

"Ugh," someone said. The rest of the class groaned in agreement.

"He gave me one week. I spent one entire weekend paging through my art history book, looking at clothes. Something kept drawing me back to the progression of women's clothing and finally I settled on the 1940s. Pinup models and actresses like Bette Davis and Ava Gardner. They wore clothes that were quite different from anything women prior to that time had worn."

There wasn't a sound in the room. I'd never had a classroom so quiet.

"Needless to say, the more I learned, the more I lost myself in my paper. I even pulled an all-nighter without even meaning to. On Monday morning, I turned the paper in. Immediately after, I went straight to my advisor's office to add a second major—*fashion*. I studied in Paris, London, New York, and finally Milan before deciding to teach."

I wanted to hear *everything* about her travels. I'd been dreaming of visiting Paris since my love for fashion had begun.

"It's my first year here at Canterwood," Ms. Snow

said. "So I've got as much to learn about the campus as any other new students."

I wished she would talk during the entire class! I wanted to hear about everything she'd ever seen.

"But that's plenty about me," Ms. Snow said. "Thank you all for indulging me. Please use the remainder of the time to work on your other studies and we'll delve into the first lesson at the next class."

Ms. Snow sat at her desk and began typing on her laptop.

I took a Post-it out of my bag and scribbled a note to Cole.

She is très *amazing!!*

I held my hand low, watching to make sure Ms. Snow didn't look up. Cole's fingers brushed mine as he took the note. He opened it under his desk and wrote something on it before reaching back toward me.

Très magnifique!

J'adore Cole for writing back in French! I took out my math book and started on the thirty assigned problems due tomorrow. Four problems were solved before I stopped midway through my work.

In less than two hours, I would I'd learn my fate on the Canterwood Crest Equestrian team!

25

DECISIONS,

DECISIONS . . .

I TOOK MY TIME WALKING FROM LAST period to my room instead of racing to spend more time at the stable.

I didn't know if I was ready for Mr. Conner's decision yet.

I opened the door to my room.

"Hey, roomie!"

"Hey, what's that—

"I made you tea!" Khloe interrupted, practically jumping up and down. "I remembered what you told me the other day about chamomile being calming? I thought you could use that before going to the stable."

"Wow! Khloe, omigosh, that was *so* sweet. I've rambled on and on to you about so much tea stuff, I can't believe you even remembered that."

Our coffee table had two steaming mugs of tea on my favorite Kate Spade coasters—pink with silver polka dots. I sat on the carpeted floor across the table from Khloe.

"I hope you're not mad that I used your stuff," she said. "I was trying to think of the thing that would make you feel the most calm and *voilá*. I thought of tea!"

"Of course not—I don't care about that stuff," I said. "Use it whenever you like. I was going to race from here to the stable, but I *knew* I needed to take a breath. This is exactly what I needed."

I blew on the hot tea and took a sip. Khloe watched me.

"How is it?" she asked, cringing a little as if she was expecting a bad response.

"Perfect," I told her. "Like you've been making tea forever."

"Thanks, Laur!" Khloe beamed. "That means a lot coming from you!"

We drank our tea and talked about the day. I told her about fashion with Ms. Snow and she told me how unfair it was that a girl in her Spanish class was already fluent.

"All I'm saying is, it totally throws off the curve," Khloe muttered, rolling her eyes.

I swallowed the last sip of tea. "Thanks again," I said. "This made me feel so much better."

"You didn't need the tea for that," Khloe said. "You're going to be fine when Mr. Conner makes the announcements. I know it."

"We'll see," I said, managing a shaky smile.

We changed into our riding clothes and left for the stable. Khloe talked the entire way—trying to distract me—but I didn't hear a word she said. I nodded when it felt right and made "mmm hmm" sounds when I thought I should, but I couldn't stop thinking about what was about to happen.

"Lauren."

"What?"

"The news is going to be good. Now go into the arena and text me when Mr. Conner's finished. I'm going to go pet Whisper for you until you're done, okay?"

I took a deep breath. "Okay. And can you scratch behind her ears? She loves that."

"I will. Now go!" Khloe gave me a gentle shove through the arena entrance.

Inside, a group of students had gathered. No one spoke to or looked at one another. I stood with fifteen or so people who all wanted the same answer I did: *You made the intermediate team.*

"Hello, everyone," Mr. Conner said, striding into the arena. His clipboard was pressed against his royal blue polo shirt. Not a chance anyone would get a peek at that list.

The group murmured a greeting back.

"I know you're all anxious for the news," Mr. Conner said. "I will not keep you waiting any further."

I felt sort of dizzy, like the arena floor was tilting under my feet. I took another long, deep breath.

"As you're aware, there is one open seat on the intermediate team," Mr. Conner said. "The decision of whom to put on that team was not an easy one. It was based on many factors, including but not limited to skill, potential growth for the rider, and his or her horse."

Please, please just say it!

"I want to thank you all for trying out. To those who did not make it, I sincerely hope you will try out again in the spring. That said, I'd like to welcome . . ."

Sounds of ocean waves crashed in my ears.

You can try out next year. Be happy you're at Canterwood. You have your dream horse. You're—

" . . . Lauren Towers to the intermediate team."

—on the intermediate team! Oh, mon Dieu!

Mr. Conner smiled at me. "Congratulations, Lauren.

The Canterwood riding board and I are pleased to welcome you to our intermediate team."

People I didn't even know patted me on the back. Some whispered, "Congratulations." It was all a blur. Once my vision cleared, I smiled back at all of them. Only now I saw the disappointment in their eyes.

"I wish the rest of you a good evening," Mr. Conner said. "I hope you know just how difficult my decision was and that I'm proud to have each and every one of you representing our stable."

The students trickled out of the arena and, once I stood alone with Mr. Conner, it started to *really* hit me.

I'd made the intermediate team.

I, Lauren Towers, rode on the intermediate team for Canterwood Crest! My phone battery was going to need serious charging—I had to call all of my friends at Union, Becca, and Mom and Dad.

"Congratulations again, Lauren," Mr. Conner said.

"Thank you, sir," I said, clenching my jaw to avoid teary eyes.

"I chose you because you're an extremely talented young rider. You've had a lot of training and have wonderful experience in the competitive circle. But, as I stated, that didn't play a role in my decision today. I considered you as if I knew nothing about your background at all. I saw a talented young rider and her horse, both of whom have the potential to grow and do very well here at Canterwood."

I smiled. "Thank you so much. Whisper and I are going to work hard, I promise. You won't regret your decision."

Mr. Conner smiled back. "Whisper is a strong, willing young mare. I look forward to coaching both of you. You'll have a lesson each afternoon unless otherwise stated. Mike and Doug will care for Whisper in the morning. Her stall, feeding, and grooming all falls to you in the evening."

"Oh, but I can feed her and muck out her stall in the morning, too," I said. "No one else has to do that for *me*!"

"Well! While I thank you for offering," Mr. Conner said, "it's stable policy for young riders. We want your focus on school in the morning. You'll have *plenty* of stable chores—trust me. And, if not, come find me and I'll be happy to give you more." He laughed heartily.

To my surprise, I started laughing too.

"Deal," I said.

"Please go ahead and groom Whisper and tack up," Mr. Conner said. "Your first lesson begins in half an hour. I'll see you in the main outdoor arena."

"Thank you," I said. "Thank you so much!"

I wanted to hug him, but I restrained myself. Instead, I half skipped out of the arena. Khloe leaned against Whisper's stall door. She and Whisper turned their heads toward me, but I didn't have to say a word.

"Oh, my God!" Khloe said. "You made it!"

She grabbed me in a fierce hug and we jumped up and down, squealing as if we were five.

Whisper's eyes widened. She tossed her head, looking at Khloe and me.

"Oh, sorry, baby girl," I said.

Khloe and I went to her head and rubbed her cheeks. "We didn't mean to scare you," Khloe said to Whisper in a soothing voice.

"I just found out that we're going to be on the intermediate team, Wisp," I said, resting my head on her neck. "You worked so hard all summer with me. I'm so proud of you."

Whisper let out a soft breath. I kissed her cheek and peered around her to see Khloe.

"Thank you for being here," I said. "Of anyone on this campus, I'm so happy I got to tell you the news first."

"Pffft. Like I could have concentrated if I'd *tried* to do anything else," Khloe said. "We'll have to have tea and a special celebratory dessert tonight."

"Sounds *great*. But right now, I've got to get Whisper groomed and tacked up. My first lesson starts in half an hour!"

"Go, go," Khloe said. "I've got a solo practice session. But I'll meet you in our room later. And I'll bring dessert!"

"Awesome. Thanks, Khlo."

We smiled at each other before splitting. I grabbed Whisper's tack and, hurrying, turned a corner smacking right into Riley.

The petite girl stumbled backward and, at the last second, got her footing back and righted herself.

"Oh, my God, I'm so sorry," I said. "Are you okay?"

"Are you unable to *read*?" Riley snapped. "There are signs everywhere saying not to run in here. It would have been just your luck if you'd injured me before show season."

"Riley, I'm really, really sorry. I'm glad you're okay and you're right—I shouldn't have been rushing."

"Whatever." Riley brushed past me. "Please don't run to your beginner lesson next time."

"Intermediate, actually," I said, letting the door close behind me.

I put Whisper's tack on an empty saddle rack.

A strawberry roan mare was being groomed in my

usual set of crossties. Instead, I tied Whisper to the iron bars on her stall. I groomed her in record time, but took enough time to make sure every hair on her body gleamed.

Whisper turned her head toward me and I used a soft cloth to wipe her delicate face with its dished muzzle. It made her look part Arabian.

Whisper seemed to feed off my excitement. She danced in place when I arranged the saddle on her back and eagerly took the snaffle bit from my hand. I put on my helmet and led Whisper through the side aisle and outside. I gathered the reins and mounted.

Whisper started off at a walk toward the arena. Lexa and Cole, already warming up, took their horses in circles.

I gave Whisper rein, letting her into a trot. We went through the entrance and Lexa and Cole looked up when they heard Whisper's hooves on the arena dirt.

"You made it!" Lexa said. "Yay! Yay!" She trotted Honor up to us.

"I still can't believe it," I said. "I'm so excited to ride with you guys!"

"Congratulations!" Cole called to me. He smiled and took Valentino through another figure eight.

"Warm up with us," Lexa suggested. "Everyone else

will be here in a few minutes. The horses have to be warmed up by the time Mr. Conner arrives."

I nodded and let Whisper trot after Honor. A good breeze blew my hair back. The cloudless sky made for an unusually mild day. We made a few laps around the arena before Clare and Riley rode in. They both stared at me and then at each other.

Clare flashed me a quick smile. "Hi, Lauren. Congrats on making the intermediate team."

"Thanks, Clare," I said.

Riley stared a long time, looking at me from Adonis's back. The gray gelding was so tall—he had to be nearly seventeen hands—and his nostrils flared pink. His ears shifted back and forth and he struck a foreleg, scraping the grass.

Whisper didn't flinch. She lifted her head, locking eyes with Adonis. That was my girl—not afraid of another horse who was obviously trying to intimidate her.

Adonis held his ground—keeping his eyes on Whisper—my eyes danced back and forth between the two of them. Just when I thought the staring contest would go on forever, Adonis snorted, shaking his head.

Riley tightened the reins. "Sorry, *Lauren*. Adonis must have picked up on my shock at seeing you here."

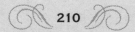

"I did tell you that I made the team," I reminded her, slightly amused.

Riley's upper lip curled. "I remember, but still. Surprised."

We looked at each other, just as the horses had done, before the sound of hoofbeats entering the arena caused us both to look up. Drew rode a blood bay gelding at a slow walk into the arena. He waved to Cole and Lexa, smiled at Clare, and then he saw me and Riley.

"Lauren!" he exclaimed, urging his horse forward. "You made it! That's *awesome!*"

"Thanks," I said, blushing.

Drew's intense dark blue eyes settled over me and his lips parted in a brilliant smile.

"We have six riders! Now we'll be able to do pairs activities," Drew said. "We should partner up sometime."

"That would be cool," I said. Okay, even *I* was feeling giddy now.

Riley cleared her throat. "Geez, Drew. Way to ignore your other teammates." She stuck out her bottom lip.

Drew looked at her. "Sorry, Riles. I wasn't ignoring you at all. Isn't it great that Lauren's on our team now?"

Riley's face, still sour, morphed into the fakest smile *ever.* "*So* awesome! I told her she'd make it. Told you, *Laur.*"

I heard a snort behind me and, when I turned, I could swear I caught Cole rolling his eyes at Lexa.

I decided not to call her out. If she wanted to be fake and lie—fine. But if Drew was as smart as he seemed, he'd see through her act.

Whisper reached her muzzle toward Drew's horse. The gelding pointed his ears in a friendly pose and touched his muzzle to Whisper's.

"What's his name?" I asked. "He's gorgeous."

"Polo," Drew said. "And thanks! I got him about a year ago. He's an Arab and Thoroughbred mix."

"I wouldn't have guessed just by temperament," I said. "He seems so calm."

"Nothing fazes him," Drew said. "That's what makes us such a great pair on the cross-country course. Polo's always up for anything."

I loved listening to Drew talk about his horse. He reminded me of the way I sounded when I talked about Whisper.

At that moment, Mr. Conner walked into the arena.

Within seconds, everyone had their horses lined up in front of him.

I'd been so excited about making the team, I'd almost forgotten—the *hard* part was only just beginning.

26

LT AND ROTTEN REILER=BFFS 4 EVA

"I HOPE YOU'VE ALL TAKEN THE TIME TO welcome our newest member to the team," Mr. Conner said.

"We did, Mr. Conner," Riley said in a sugary voice. "And we'll help Lauren with any questions she might have. I *know* she'll fit right in."

"Wonderful," Mr. Conner said, nodding at Riley. "Glad to hear it."

Next to me, Lexa made a barely audible grumble.

"Let's get right to today's lesson," Mr. Conner said. "We're going to spend this session on flatwork exercises. It'll be a warm-up for lessons to follow, and it'll give me a chance to see how you've all progressed over the summer."

This was it. My first official lesson at Canterwood.

My inner cheesiness wished I had my digital camera to take a snapshot of this moment.

"Take your horses to the wall," Mr. Conner said. "Leaving plenty of space between each other. Follow my direction when it's given."

I got into line behind Cole and in front of Lexa. I took a breath, reminding myself that this was practice—not a show.

"Trot," Mr. Conner called.

The six of us let our horses trot. I posted easily and Whisper stayed the perfect distance behind Polo. She knew not to tailgate. Lexa and Honor did the same.

"Cross through the center and trot in the opposite direction," Mr. Conner said.

Clare, at the front of the line, crossed first. Fuego, her gelding, moved beautifully. The liver chestnut had long, lean legs and a strong back. I loved his stripe. Drew went after Clare and I followed him with Lexa and Cole behind us.

We trotted around the arena twice before Mr. Conner asked us to walk.

"Cross your stirrup irons over your saddle," he said. "Then move into a sitting trot."

This was *not* my favorite exercise, but at least he hadn't

asked for the two worst ones—making us stand in the stirrups and keep our balance without tugging on our horse's mouth or lapping the arena while crouched in the two-point position. After doing those at Kim's, I'd always needed to soak in the bathtub for hours afterward.

I let Whisper trot and sat without a problem to her smooth stride. We moved around the arena and Mr. Conner raised his hand, signaling us to stop.

"Put your stirrups back in place, change directions, and trot," he said.

Whisper's ears flicked back and forth as we changed with Lexa in front of us again.

"Canter," Mr. Conner said.

Whisper bolted forward into an unsteady canter. Caught off guard, she threw me backward, jostling my right boot almost out of the stirrup. I sat deep in the saddle, applying pressure to the reins and bringing her to a trot. I readjusted my position.

My face burned.

I thought we'd had this problem corrected over the summer. Whisper responded immediately, slowing to a trot. But Drew cantered Polo around us, followed by Riley and Clare. Riley probably couldn't wait for the lesson to be over so she could laugh about my mistake.

"Good call to make her trot, Lauren," Mr. Conner said. "Now, ask her to change gaits again."

I slid my leg behind the girth, asking Whisper to canter. Within two strides, she moved into a canter.

Every ounce of my focus was on Whisper for the rest of the lesson. She was an angel while Mr. Conner worked with us. We worked through basic exercises and right when I felt like we were really in a groove, Mr. Conner held up his hand, signaling us to come to the center. I ended up next to Riley. She reached over and patted my arm.

Ew! Had she really just touched me?!

"Don't worry, Lauren," Riley said. Her tone was low enough so that Mr. Conner, who was still making notes, couldn't hear. "I'm sure Mr. Conner won't take you off the intermediate team just because you made one really dumb mistake on the first day."

I didn't look at her.

Mr. Conner would *never*. And cattiness was just *so* not my scene.

"Great first practice, *everyone*," Mr. Conner said. "Remember, this is practice. Mistakes will be made. It's the reason why you're all here."

I could have sworn he looked at Riley for the briefest of seconds when he said that last sentence.

"Each day will be a new chance. To work out kinks, become stronger riders, bond as a team, and *work* so that when we do compete, you're connected. You trust each other. I *hope* to see you make mistakes and learn from them."

I twisted Whisper's mane in my fingers.

"If you're not making mistakes, you're either not pushing yourself to try more difficult moves or you're afraid to look bad in front of your teammates. Those are riders who should think carefully about their place on this team."

Mr. Conner looked at each of us. "Please dismount and thoroughly cool your horses. I'll see you at tomorrow's lesson."

27

HEAD?
MEET DESK.

"LAUR? LAUR?" SOMEONE RUBBED MY shoulder.

"Huh?" I lifted my head from my desk, my vision blurry. I rubbed my eyes. "I just closed my eyes for a sec. I have math and science—then I'm done."

I sat up in my desk chair. My homework was spread across my desk. Then I looked back at Khloe. Pretty, wide-awake Khloe in jeans, wedges, and a deep purple lacey cami with a dark gray cardigan.

"Why are you dressed?" I asked, more awake now.

Khloe leaned against the wall. "I'm dressed for class. Lauren, it's time to get ready! You must have fallen asleep at your desk last night."

"What?! No." I glanced at the clock. Seven forty. *A.m.*

"Omigod. Omigod. Khloe, how could I have fallen asleep? I didn't finish my homework! I have math *first period*." I flipped furiously through my notebook, some pages beginning to tear.

"Hey." Khloe gently pushed my hands away and took the book. "Hey, it happens. I'll be in class with you. Maybe you could turn in the problems you have and then ask for make-up work. Ms. Utz won't be mean about it."

I rubbed my face in my hands—mascara coming off on my hands. I hadn't showered after my lesson yesterday. When I'd gotten back, I realized I had so much work to do that I'd thrown on my loungey clothes and decided to tackle some homework before showering. At dinnertime, I was deep into history homework. I'd told Khloe to go on without me, even though she said she'd wait. I'd never made it to the cafeteria.

My stomach rumbled as a reminder.

Khloe put a glass of OJ and a blueberry muffin in front of me. "Eat that," she said. "I tried to wake you up, but you were *out*. There's no time to hit the caf for breakfast, but at least it's something."

"I'm so sorry," I said. "Did you eat?"

"I had a muffin, too," Khloe said. "And stop

apologizing! Want me to get your papers and stuff put away so you can get cleaned up and dressed?"

Khloe was right—I had no time to even finish the last ten math problems. During lunch, I'd be able to do science since it was my last class today.

I *hated* this. I was not this girl. I'd never turned in anything half-completed. It was only the third day of classes—making a good impression on my new teachers was important to me.

"Please," I finally said. "Thank you, Khlo. I really appreciate it."

"You're welcome. Don't worry about it."

I was so upset about my homework, I didn't even care what I wore. That was a first, too. I grabbed plain, boot-cut jeans and a hunter green scoop-neck T-shirt. With the bathroom door shut behind me, I looked in the mirror.

I had notebook paper lines on my right cheek, a pencil smudge on my nose, and my eyes were bloodshot. Mascara had smeared under my eyes—making my already dark circles that much darker.

I scrubbed my face, applied moisturizer, brushed my hair, and pulled it into a ponytail. I brushed my teeth and finished dressing.

I came out, tossed yesterday's clothes on my bed and

saw my bag all packed. I smiled my thanks at Khloe and started eating.

"Did you have a crazy load of homework yesterday?" Khloe asked. She stood in front of our full-length mirror, making last-minute waves in her hair with a curling iron.

"I had a lot, but I think I was exhausted from worrying so much about my first lesson. There was no other reason I couldn't have finished it."

Khloe wrapped a piece of long blond hair around the iron. "I hate hearing you beat yourself up about it. I promise—Ms. Utz's is going to be fine. Just remember what we talked about before classes started."

She turned off the iron and I swallowed the last of my OJ. Right—Khloe had cautioned me about taking too many courses.

"I will."

I looked over my schedule, reminding myself about today's glee club auditions. After that, I had riding and probably another full night of homework. I wasn't surprised—I'd known it would take me a while to adjust to Canterwood's pace.

Khloe just didn't know me well enough yet.

She and Lexa had been concerned about my courses, but I knew I could do it. I'd signed up for all my classes

to impress the teachers and prove to everyone that Canterwood had made the right decision by admitting me.

Okay, I'd messed up last night. But it would *never* happen again. Khloe and Lexa would see that I was more than capable of handling my schedule.

We left Hawthorne and hurried to get to math on time. Lexa, already seated, smiled when she saw us.

Khloe and I took the seats she'd saved for us and we'd just sat down when Ms. Utz walked in, closing the door behind her.

After attendance, Ms. Utz moved to the front of the room.

"Please pass your homework forward and we'll begin today's lesson," she said. I handed off my paper and kept my eyes down for the rest of the period.

"Remember to finish reading the chapter and complete tonight's thirty homework problems," Ms. Utz said. "See you tomorrow."

The bell rang and I realized I hadn't taken a single note. I'd spent the entire class thinking about what to say to Ms. Utz about my homework. Luckily, I hadn't been called to the board to solve any problems during class.

Lexa and Khloe stood, waiting for me.

"You guys go," I said. "I have to talk to Ms. Utz. I'll catch up with you later."

"BBM me," Khloe mouthed. She gave me an *it's going to be fine* look and left with Lexa.

I took my time gathering my stuff as the room emptied. Once the last student had left, I slung my bag over my shoulder and walked up to Ms. Utz's desk.

"Hi, Ms. Utz," I said. "May I speak with you for a moment?"

"Hi, Lauren. Of course," she said. "What's on your mind?"

I opened my mouth, pausing. It was hard to get out the words. "I turned in my homework, but it's not finished. I'm sorry. Is there any chance for extra credit or some sort of make-up work that I can do to keep up my grade?"

Ms. Utz frowned. "Lauren, I appreciate you coming to me directly. However, there are no extensions or make-up work given in this class to make up for missed or late homework."

I felt sick.

This had never happened to me. Ever. At Yates, I'd looked at the students who turned in unfinished or zero work without sympathy. Now here I was.

"I'm so sorry," I said. "I stayed up—"

"Excuses don't help your grade," Ms. Utz said. "Instead, turn in your homework on time. I recognize it's your first year at Canterwood, but you've had all summer to prepare."

"You're right," I said. "There are no excuses. I won't miss another assignment."

"Good," Ms. Utz said. "The schedule will become much more intense as the semester wears on, so please make sure you're on top of it."

"Of course," I said. "Thank you for talking to me."

Ms. Utz nodded and I left the classroom, rushing to history. I bit the inside of my cheek to keep myself from crying.

Before I walked into Mr. Spellman's class, I took a breath. *You're not feeling sorry for yourself all day. You missed one assignment and it'll never happen again.*

I walked into the classroom with my head high. Whatever assignments I walked away with at the end of the day would be completed, done well, and on time.

Like the two days before it, Wednesday's classes rushed by.

I skipped lunch, downing two cups of green tea instead, and spent the period finishing my science homework. I didn't even have time to talk to Khloe about glee.

I dropped my heavy book bag in our room, grabbed riding clothes to change into at the stable, and swung by the common room. I made a quick thermos of iced tea, grabbed a snack bar, and headed out.

"Lauren?" called Christina, my dorm monitor, poking her head out of her office.

I knew they'd put her office right by the front door on purpose!

My stomach tightened. "Yes?" I stopped and took a too-big gulp of tea.

"Everything okay?" she asked. "I saw you run in and you've moving around marathon-style a lot lately."

"Never better," I lied. "I got out of class a little late and am heading to an audition for glee club now. I hate being late."

"Okay," Christina said. She stared for a second, looking as if she was trying to decide whether or not to believe me. "But promise you'll let me know if you need anything, though."

"Promise!" I gave her a huge smile and made sure I walked at a normal pace out the door. Once I got to the sidewalk, I sprinted toward the media center. It was one of the few buildings I hadn't been inside of yet, but it sounded amazing from the descriptions online.

I followed signs to the media center, dodging clusters of students who'd stopped to talk and some who walked so slow, it looked as if they weren't moving at all. If they tried to walk like that in Brooklyn, they'd be in serious trouble!

I walked the final steps up the sidewalk and climbed a few stairs to the auditorium door. A blast of cold air hit me when I opened the door and, once inside, I stopped.

Wow.

I'd heard the media center was cool, but I'd had no idea it would look like *this*! Directly in front of me was a section of couches and plasma TVs. There were built-in bookcases of hundreds—maybe thousands—of DVDs. Vending machines were in each corner of the room. A hallway went off to the left and students carrying DVDs, popcorn, and other movie-snacks walked down the hall.

I checked my watch—there were a couple of minutes to explore. I followed the students down the hallway and passed room after room set up for private TV viewing or gaming. Each room had a Blu-ray player and several gaming consoles from the Wii to the Xbox. Each of the rooms had a different setup with various paint colors, couches, and recliners in different spots.

I walked back down the hallway to the main entrance. Ahead of me were doors . . . to a movie theater! *Oh, mon Dieu!* I had to show Becca right this instant. I looked around to make sure no one was watching (I didn't want to look like a dork!) and snapped a photo of the room with my BlackBerry.

I typed a quick message and sent it with the photo. *Becs! CC's media center is insane! Look @ the concession stand!!*

Becca is typing a message. While I waited for her reply, I looked at the students lined up for movie snacks. There were showtimes on a digital board near the entrance. A new action flick with Jared Tyler Smith, a *très* cute actor, started in ten minutes. Behind the concessions counter, students filled soda cups and popcorn buckets and handed out candy.

I'm so bringing Khloé here this weekend! I thought. Then I frowned. It depended on how much homework I got done.

My phone buzzed.

Becca: !!! I am so jealous. I hate u! ;) JK. It looks amazing! U there 4 glee?

Lauren: Yep. Abt 2 go in now. Just wanted u 2 c.

Becca: I ♥ *it & you're going 2 do awesome! BBM me.*

Lauren: I will. ♥

I put away my phone, happy that I'd talked to my sister

before my audition. Today hadn't been the best day, and sharing something with Becca made me feel good.

I paused in front of a giant wooden door with a sign taped to it.

GLEE CLUB AUDITIONS. PLEASE ENTER QUIETLY.

I eased open the heavy door and blinked to adjust to the different lighting. Beside me, a girl sitting at a banquet table waved me over. She was tiny and sweet-looking, with dimples and blond spiral curls, which were pushed back with a skinny gold plastic headband with tiny teeth that combed the hair away from her heart-shaped face.

"Hi, I'm Melissa Peeples," she said. "Are you trying out for glee club?"

"Yeah. Hi—I'm Lauren," I said, returning her infectious smile.

"Welcome, Lauren! I'm the glee club cocaptain! We're always excited to see new people audition. Just fill out this info sheet and pass it back to me when you're done."

"Thanks."

I took the paper and pen that Melissa gave me and filled out the form.

Name: Lauren Towers

Grade: 7

Previous experience: 1 year in glee club at Yates Preparatory, frequent shower singer

Song choice: "Seasons of Love" from Rent

I handed the paper back to Melissa and she scanned it. "Thanks! And *no way!* Rent is only like the best musical *ever!* Insanely good audition piece."

"Thanks!" I said. I wondered if Melissa was also captain of the cheer squad. She might have been the nicest, most bubbly person I'd ever met. "It's my favorite song, too."

"You came at the *perfect* time. If you want to head downstage, I'll give your info to Mr. Harrison, our glee club advisor. You can audition now!"

Melissa disappeared, and I stood for a minute, rolling my shoulders back, tilting my head up high, and reminding myself to breathe before walking down the aisle.

The auditorium and spotlit stage felt much bigger than when I'd been here for Headmistress Drake's first-day assembly. I'd wanted more time to prep, but maybe this would help me beat stage fright.

My phone buzzed in my back pocket. I pulled it out, glad it had done that now and *not* while I was onstage! I set it to silent and read the new BBM.

Khloe: BREAK A LEG!!

I smiled at my roomie's thoughtfulness and *freakishly* good timing. I put my phone in the back pocket of my skinny jeans and climbed the small set of stairs to the stage.

An X was marked with black tape on the floor. I walked to my mark. Behind me, a pianist sat at a grand piano. I walked over to tell him the song I'd chosen, and he smiled at me. "I know it well," he assured me. He smiled again, and then I walked back to my spot.

The lights changed, dimming around me so I wasn't blinded, but I still had to hold my hand over my forehead like a visor to see Mr. Harrison. He was young, like Ms. Snow, with thinning light brown hair.

"Hello, Lauren," he called. "My name is Mr. Harrison. I am the faculty advisor for Canterwood's glee club, Vocal Harmony."

"Hello," I replied.

"And you will be performing 'Seasons of Love'?"

"Correct." I smiled.

"Wonderful," he said with a warm smile. "Please begin when you're ready."

I nodded. My heart rate sped up and I felt an adrenaline rush. But I kept my breathing in control and waited for my cue. While I sang the lyrics to a song about

endless, timeless love, I thought about my family—Becca, especially—and Whisper. At the song's end, I blinked away tears and smiled at Mr. Harrison. "Thank you," I said.

"Lauren," he said, "the pleasure was mine. That was an excellent sound choice for your voice. The meaning of the song seemed to resonate with you. You have a lovely voice."

"Thank you," I said.

"Welcome to Vocal Harmony!" Mr. Harrison said, grinning. "Congratulations!"

"YES!" came a shout from the balcony. Mr. Harrison turned around to look,

I put my hand over my forehead and squinted to see. Had there been other Vocal Harmony people listening in?

"You rock, LT!" There was a flash of long blond hair, and then she was gone.

Khloe.

"Friend of yours?" Mr. Harrison asked, clearly amused.

"Um, perhaps an *ex*-friend," I joked. I couldn't decide whether to kill her or hug her.

"I'll see you next week on Wednesday for rehearsal," he said. "And your cheering squad"—he raised his voice— "should be very proud of her talented *ex*-friend."

I laughed, thanked him again, and rushed offstage.

Khloe and I reached the center of the lobby at the same time. She was already dressed for riding in navy breeches, boots, and a T-shirt.

"Yaaay!" Khloe squealed. "Lauren! I'm so proud of my 'ex-friend.'" She laughed.

"I can't believe it!" I hugged her, then shoved her. "How long were you up there?"

"Long enough to know that Melissa needs some *major* cheering up. She seriously seems depressed!"

Even I had to laugh at that one.

Khloe approached a girl and boy—definitely high school students—who were headed into the theater.

"OMG! Khloe!" But it was too late. I put my hand over my eyes, spreading my fingers just enough to see a tiny bit.

"My roomie, Lauren." She pointed at me, and I felt my face go watermelon pink. "She just got into glee club! *And* she rides horses! *And* speaks French! *And?* Boys *luuurve* her!"

My watermelon face turned into a tomato.

"I'm not kidding," she told them, laughing. "Boy *magnet*. We're going to celebrate! By the way, my name is Khloe Kinsella, and you have just been given a PSA about my new roommate. And," she said, with a serious and sincere expression, "she is my new best friend."

"Congratulations," the older girl said. "Enjoy your celebration with your new BFF." She winked at me, heading inside. "And nice to meet you, Khloe Kinsella!" she shouted.

"Khlo!" I said, laughing harder and harder. "They were probably *sophomores!*"

She rolled her eyes. "Please. I'm so happy for you that I would have said the same to the headmistress herself."

I looked at her, an eyebrow arched.

"Okay," Khloe said, rolling her eyes playfully. "Maybe not the *headmistress.*"

"I have to text my sister!" I said. "She'll be so excited that I got into glee!"

I sent Becca a BBM. *Made it!!!* ☺ *First glee club practice is nxt Weds!*

Becca, really the best sister ever, must have been waiting by her phone. *KNEW IT! YAY! So proud of u, LaurBell. Do u want 2 tell Mom & Dad?*

Lauren: Mom & Dad. Tell them. Riding lesson. Tell them I'll call ltr.

Becca: Will do. OK. Have a good lesson ☺☺ *Mom & Dad will b so xcited!*

I locked my phone and my eyes misted. "I wish you could meet Becca."

Khloe smiled. "If she comes to Family Day, we have to meet. Know about Family Day?"

We turned down the sidewalk. "No," I said. "What is it?" A slight breeze picked up. The scent of horses, hay, and freshly cut grass wafted through the air.

"It's late in the fall," Khloe said. "Parents, siblings, grandparents, et cetera, come visit. It's usually the first Friday of November. The family gets to shadow the student. Please note: The food in the caf gets mysteriously better the very week of Family Day. Coincidence? I think not."

Khloe and I laughed.

"Last year," Khloe said, "I was so excited to see my mom and dad. They got here, met my roommate, and came to science class with me. Then my lab partner passed me a note. Dad saw the note and 'whispered' to me about it. Side note? My father damaged his hearing when he was young and at war. Roadside bomb, thank God no one got hurt . . . well, except his eardrums. So now he's superloud about everything."

"What did he say?" I asked.

"Nothing. He *yelled*, 'You like this boy? He passes you notes in class?'"

My mouth dropped open.

Khloe continued, "So, after the whole class finished

laughing *hysterically*—oh, and did I mention that *yes*, I was crushing on him?"

"Oh, Khlo . . . ," I said, "What'd you do? Who was it?"

"Well, I stood up, unfolded the note, and said, 'Hi, everyone. I'm about to read something my father wants to hear."

"You didn't!"

"Sure did," she said. "So I read it. 'KK: Do you have any extra paper? I ran out.' Really romantic, huh, Dad?"

"No!" I said, giggling.

"I got sent to the headmistress's office. And when I got there and explained what had happened word for word? She stared at me for thirty whole seconds before laughing like a hyena for five then ten minutes. So, see? No matter how much you love your family . . ."

"Be prepared for disaster on Family Day."

Khloe nodded.

"Oh, Khlo. Who," I asked my new BFF, "was the guy?"

Khloe *blushed*. She covered her face with both hands. "Drew Adams."

28

MISS YOU, LOVE YOU, MEAN IT!

BACK IN MY ROOM I ERASED AN ANSWER ON my multiple-choice English take-home quiz for the sixth time. I rubbed so hard, a hole appeared in the paper.

"Ugh," I groaned, tossing my pencil down and massaging my scalp. (Dad always did it soo well—mine was puny compared to the awesome scalp massages he gave me. Mom said it's one of the reasons she married him.)

Khloe played with the edges of her script. "Have you thought about seeing the guidance counselor?"

"Why would I do that?" I asked.

"You're so stressed over classes, and you have every right to be—you're taking a *lot* of advanced ones. I know I keep bringing it up, but have you thought about dropping any?"

"Not once," I said. "I expected classes to be this hard! It's only the first week. Soon I'll figure out how to balance everything."

"It *is* the first week," Khloe said. "And you've been up all night once, and it seems like you will be again tonight. I wish you'd have time to enjoy Canterwood a little, too."

"I am. I just made glee club! And the riding team is great. I promise, if I still feel overwhelmed in a week or two, I'll go talk to Ms. Utz."

Khloe smiled. "Good." She went back to reading her script.

When my phone buzzed on my desk, I answered instantly.

"Bri!"

"Laur!"

I wanted to hug her through the phone.

"Why does your phone sound all echoey?" I asked.

She laughed. "You caught me. I just finished homework and I'm putting the finishing touches on my new clean room."

Brielle and I had been two of a kind—both neat freaks and overachievers. I felt like I was there in her room. I could smell the vanilla cupcake candles she always burned. I imagined lying on her bed, our stomachs down, our feet

wrapped behind us as we watched *Sin City Celebutantes*.

"I miss you so much," Bri said. "I'm so glad we're finally on the phone."

"Me too. And it's only been a couple of days!"

"How's everything?" Bri asked. "You sound . . . *meh*."

"Meh" was the word we'd all come up with at Union to describe a bad mood when we didn't even know where it came from.

And Brielle was right—I felt "meh."

"Well," I finally said, "I had a bad riding lesson today."

"What happened?" Brielle asked.

"Whisper started responding to verbal cues again. She cantered when Mr. Conner said 'canter,' and today she trotted when he said 'trot.' Remember how she did that over the summer?"

"Right," Brielle said. "You and Kim worked with her on that. She started up again?"

I rubbed my forehead. "Yes! And I don't even know *when* she's going to do it, and she'll catch me off guard every time. It throws off everyone's focus during the lesson. I don't know what to do."

Bri was quiet for a moment. "Remember what you and Kim did together?"

"Kim called verbal commands and I made sure Whisper

waited for my signals and if she didn't, I held her to another gait."

"Have you tried that?"

"Not in my lesson," I said. "There are five other people who are there to learn."

"What about someone from your class?"

I turned my head to look at Khloe. "Khlo, do you have any free time this week?"

"I thought you'd never ask," Khloe said, clearly having eavesdropped the whole time. "Of course I'll help."

I smiled at her and then turned back to the phone. "Thanks, Bri. That was a genius idea. I'm going to work with Whisper and kick that habit."

"I know you can," Brielle said. "You did it before. You know, I'm glad I called you."

"Me too. So, what's going on at Yates?"

"Oh. My. God. *So* much. You won't believe it! So, Ana and Jeremy are, like, totally into each other. Seriously. It's PDA every five seconds! You'd be so grossed out. And plus, Will is . . ."

I let Brielle talk until she ran out of breath. Everything she said made me miss home and Yates. I wasn't there to see Ana and her first boyfriend. I wouldn't see Tay's swim meets. Brielle and I wouldn't be shopping together. The

three of us used to know every bit of school gossip. We were on the inside. Now, I was barely keeping my head above water.

Finally, I stopped Bri by saying I had a lot of homework to do, which *was* true. We hung up and I went back to work. This time, I was able to concentrate because I finally had a plan for Whisper.

I was *not* going to use my desk as a pillow tonight.

29

E-VITATION
AND TGIT

7:12 a.m.: TGIT

It's only Thursday, but I'm grateful for that! This week has been so intense that I'm basically counting down the minutes until the end of classes tomorrow. I managed to finish all of my homework last night and I woke up early this morning with time to blog.

The two things I'm looking forward to the most today?

1. Fashion class.

2. Riding. Duh!

I've got a lesson and then K's going to help me with Whisper.

Oh! When I finished talking to B last night, K and I talked about what a long first week it had been. We decided to have a . . . wait for it . . . sleepover on Friday night. K volunteered to send e-vites today. The only bad part? We have to invite R. K obviously wants C to come and we can't not ask R. Hopefully, she won't want to come and she'll say no. On the invite list: C, R, L, and J.

Posted by Lauren Towers

30

BEWARE OF SHARKS
IN INDOOR POOLS

TWEEEET!

The whistle blew and I pushed off with my toes, diving into the pool. I slid into the cool water and began racing toward the opposite end of my lane. Today, Mr. Warren had us swimming relays. Through my goggles, I could see Riley in the lane next to mine, matching me stroke for stroke.

I squeezed my eyes shut so I'd stop looking at her and pushed myself, my lungs burning. I kicked harder and after two more strokes, I opened my eyes. My fingertips touched the end of the pool and I lifted my head, breathing hard. Next to me, Riley yanked off her goggles.

"Excellent, everyone," Mr. Warren said. "Lauren, you reached the end just a second before Riley, followed by Drew Adams."

I grinned.

Riley traced the top of the water with her fingertips. "Wow, good one. Maybe you should switch to the swim team instead of riding, LT. You're definitely a better swimmer than you are an equestrian."

"Maybe I should do both, Riley. I'll think about it!" I smiled at her and swam to the stairs to get out of the water. The swim had loosened my muscles and it had taken tension out of my shoulders. I'd been thinking about this afternoon—riding with Khloe—all day. I felt a little nervous. Khloe was on the advanced team. I wasn't. She didn't know about my show circuit past, championship titles, or my accident. I wanted her to see me as a good rider. A feeling I hadn't felt in a *very* long time bubbled at the surface: *competitiveness.*

But I knew better than to be competitive with Khloe. She was my roommate and fast becoming a good friend. Sometimes, though, I couldn't think about her riding on the advanced team—doing dressage moves that I'd used to do every day. Moves that, now, I couldn't let anyone see.

31

INSTRUCTOR KHLOE

AT THE STABLE KHLOE HEADED TO EVER'S stall while I went to change. I almost rounded the corner when hearing sniffling. I stopped. I didn't want to intrude on whoever was upset.

"I love him so much," a girl's voice whispered. "I want to be there for him."

It took one moment, but then the familiar voice eventually registered. *Riley.*

She murmured one last thing I couldn't make out, then moved, her boots tapping on the concrete. I left quickly, but we saw each other anyway.

Riley looked at me, mascara smudged around her eyes. "What?" she accused.

"Just heading to the bathroom to change," I said, trying to be cool.

But once I was all dressed, I couldn't stop wondering what—or who—she'd been talking about.

Riley definitely had a secret.

After our riding lessons, Khloe and I met at the small arena behind the stable. We were both on foot, leading our horses with one hand and sipping sodas with the other.

"Thanks again for offering to help," I said. "I totally owe you a trip to The Slice."

Khloe took a long sip of Diet Orange Zest and nodded. "You do. I think I'll take you up on that tonight."

"Sounds good to me. I'm dying for pizza and the restaurant sounds cute."

"It is. Plus, their pizza is so good. You'll never want Pizza Hut again."

We walked the horses through the entrance and stopped at the fence. Khloe and I climbed it, sitting on the top rail next to each other. Khloe put Ever's reins over the mare's head and let go.

"Aren't you afraid she'll wander away?" I asked.

"Nah," Khloe said. "She always stays nearby."

Khloe was right. Ever took a few steps to inspect a

yellow and black butterfly, reaching her black muzzle toward it. The butterfly flew away, toward the setting sun, and Khloe and I smiled as Ever ambled back over and nuzzled Whisper.

I took a sip of my orange soda and loosened my hold on Whisper's reins so she could reach Ever. I loved her so much and she'd been *perfect* in today's lesson, but I couldn't wait until we had a relationship like Khloe and Ever's. One of complete trust and an unbreakable connection with the other. I wanted to let Whisper loose, too, but I didn't know if the mare would head for the arena's exit.

We finished our sodas and tossed them in the trash can behind us. The temperature had cooled in the twenty something minutes we'd sat on the fence. Both horses swished their tails, standing together.

"How was your lesson?" Khloe asked, swinging her legs back and forth.

"Great," I said. "We did flatwork—exercises like spirals and serpentines. Mr. Conner said we're going to spend the rest of the week taking it easy to get the horses used to daily lessons. Next week, we're starting normal classes." I grinned. "Jumping and dressage. I can't wait to work though dressage with Whisper."

"I bet," Khloe said. "I feel the same way. Mr. Conner's making us ease into lessons. Ever's probably missing dressage as much as I am."

"I can't wait to see you two in the dressage arena," I said. "I'd like to come watch your lesson sometime, if that's okay."

Khloe smiled. "I'd love that. I wish we were in the same class, but at least we can watch each other ride sometimes. We should practice together during the weekends, if you want."

The competitive vibe I'd felt pulsing through my body evaporated. Khloe wasn't competition. She was my friend and roommate. I was embarrassed that I'd even felt the slightest bit of competitiveness when I thought about riding with her. Khloe was here, offering to help, and I just knew she wasn't looking at me as a rider beneath her.

I looked at our horses, blowing into each other's muzzles. I wanted to be honest with her. But I couldn't. Not yet.

"We definitely have to ride together," I said. "I'd love that. We should trail ride this weekend."

"And invite Cole and Lexa. It would be the perfect ending to our sleepover."

"Did you get RSVPs yet?" I crossed my fingers that Riley had said no.

"Everyone texted me back a yes," Khloe answered. "Including Lady Edwards."

We exchanged looks.

"Maybe she'll be nice since we extended an invite to her. Lexa, Clare, and Jill will be there, so at least we won't be alone with her."

Khloe hopped off the fence, her boots making a small puff of dust when she landed. "I *doubt* she'll be nice, but you're right—it won't just be the three of us. It's worth inviting her to have Clare over."

Khloe put on her helmet, and I got off the fence and did the same. Khloe didn't like talking about Clare and Riley. I wondered if it made her sad that her bestie friend was best friends with someone she couldn't stand.

"I was thinking that we could do the same exercises you did with Whisper over the summer," Khloe said.

"Sounds great. I'm ready."

We mounted and Khloe moved Ever to the center of the arena. "I'm going to keep her still and call out instructions like I'm Mr. Conner. I'll ride with you after a while."

"Good idea. I think riding with us is smart—it'll add pressure to Whisper. Plus, she's never worked with Ever before."

"Exactly. Sometimes I'm going to give commands

with a different inflection in my voice like I'm talking to Whisper."

"Perfect, Khloe."

I walked Whisper to the edge of the arena. She was already warmed up and loose from our lesson earlier.

"Trot," Khloe said. She used a tone as if she was lunging a horse—her word had an edge of command to it.

Whisper didn't respond to Khloe. She walked until I squeezed my legs tighter against her sides. I posted, rising and falling with her shoulder.

"Canter," Khloe said.

Again, Whisper didn't even flick an ear in Khloe's direction. I slid my boot behind her girth and nudged her side. I could have drifted asleep to her smooth canter. Khloe called out various commands, but Whisper didn't respond.

Khloe edged Ever out of the center of the arena and joined Whisper and me as we cantered.

"Trot," Khloe said, her voice louder over the two sets of hoofbeats.

Whisper's ears flicked back and she slowed. Before I could push her forward, she changed gaits to a fast trot.

Khloe, on purpose, let Ever canter around us. Whisper's ears flicked back and forth as she eyed Ever. The mare's black tail streamed behind her as the distance

between her and Whisper lengthened with each stride. I held Whisper to a trot and she fought my hands, the reins rubbing on her neck, as she strained to catch Ever.

"Canter," Khloe called.

I was ready. Whisper yanked her head up, trying to get more rein, but I didn't give up an inch. My legs stayed loose around her sides and I pushed myself deeper into the saddle. Whisper snorted, tossing her head in frustration. I held firm, not giving her what she wanted. Khloe and Ever lapped us and I kept Whisper to a trot. It took a few more laps before Whisper settled and I let her canter.

Khloe and I slowed the horses to a walk when the floodlights came on.

"Let's call it a night," Khloe said.

I smiled, patting Whisper's neck. "Good place to stop. Thanks again, Khlo."

"It was fun." Khloe swung her leg over Ever's saddle and lowered herself to the ground. "Whisper's such a beautiful mover."

I dismounted. "I think so, too. And you're so lucky with Ever—the bond you two have is rare."

Smiling, we led our horses out of the arena. My session with Khloe had gone better than I'd imagined and I couldn't wait for my next lesson.

32

STEP AWAY FROM
THE COFFEE

I KNELT NEXT TO A LIGHTLY SNORING KHLOE. I'd been up for hours already, doing homework. I'd managed to finish everything and, determined not to be sleepy, I'd switched to coffee. The bitter liquid had tasted *disgusting* even with heaps of Splenda, but it had kept me awake. Wide awake.

"Khloooeee," I whispered. "Khlo. Khloe."

Khloe cracked open an eye. "Lauren. What are you doing?"

She buried deeper under her covers.

"It's Friday. Sleepover day! Last day of school before the weekend. I've been up forever. It's sunny outside and the perfect day for a lesson and—"

Khloe sat up, her blond hair static-y from her

pillow. "Lauren. How many cups of tea did you have this morning?"

"Tea? No tea! I had *coffee*! I never drink coffee. Ev-er."

Khloe rubbed her eyes, laughing. "Um, no more for you. Ev-er."

I sat still for a minute, realizing it was the first time I'd been this stationary all morning. "Oops," I said, giggling. "I guess I had a little too much caffeine. I'm so sorry I woke you up!"

Khloe looked at the clock and pressed a button. "My alarm was going to go off in five minutes, anyway. I'm glad it's Friday, too. Hey, you survived your first week!"

"Almost," I said. "One more day. I'm really looking forward to tonight."

"I will be," Khloe said, rubbing her forehead. "After I audition."

"You've been working on your lines every free second. You know everything about *Beauty and the Beast*. There's nothing you can do to be more prepared."

"Yeah, well, Riley wants it, too. She's a good actress and she's been in my face about every chance she gets."

"I'm sorry. You don't deserve that. It's just like riding with her. But you know how talented you are. Don't let her psych you out."

"You're right," Khloe said. She took a big breath. "Let's get ready, get through classes and make it to the fun stuff."

Getting through classes was exactly what I did. I went from class to class, engrossed in the material. It kept me from fixating on tonight's sleepover. Except for in between classes. It was my first social event at Canterwood. I didn't even care anymore about Riley—I just wanted to hang out with the girls. I'd gotten a lot of homework done in last period—study hall—so tonight was all about having fun. It felt good to be caught up with homework and knowing I wouldn't spend the night at my desk.

Between my classes, I updated my Chatter status. *LaurBell: Sleepover 2nite! So xcited!* ☺

I got a response, minutes later, from Taylor. *TFrost: Have fun! Skype me this wkend.*

His reply made me smile. I couldn't wait to "see" him over Skype. I adjusted my backpack and left the English building, typing a response.

LaurBell: I will! Can't wait 2 talk.

I changed clothes in record time and hurried to the stable. I couldn't wait to get in the arena and see if my practice session with Khloe would help during today's lesson.

"Lauren!"

I stopped and Cole waved at me.

"Hey," I said. "What's up?"

Cole grinned. "I heard you made glee club. Congratulations!"

"Thanks! I can't wait for next week's first practice."

"Me either."

"You're in glee, too?"

"Yep," Cole said. "I auditioned at the last minute. I have bad stage fright, but I've always wanted to do something like glee club."

"Auditioning was definitely scary. What convinced you to do it?"

We reached the stable entrance and stood off to the side so we could keep talking.

"More like *who* convinced me," Cole said. "Lexa told me that to try it it was something I really wanted. I tried to talk myself out of it by saying I hadn't practiced a song. When I made that argument to Lexa, she said it was better to get up there without having too much time to think about it."

"So you did."

"I did *not* sound even remotely prepared, but Mr. Harrison said if I worked hard he'd accept me. I promised

I would. Now I'll be seeing you every Wednesday."

"That's so cool, Cole," I said. "I'm not the best singer either, trust me. We'll get better together."

We went into the stable and gathered our tack to ready Whisper and Valentino for our lesson. I tacked up Whisper, put on my helmet, and walked her to the indoor arena. I reached the entrance at the same time as Clare and Riley. Clare's red curls were back in a low ponytail under her helmet and she wore an off-the-shoulder T-shirt with a light pink tank top underneath. Riley hadn't put on her helmet yet. She looked ready for a show in tall boots, white breeches, and a button-down shirt.

Say something nice, I told myself. Something to set the mood for a good night.

"I'm glad you both were free to sleep over tonight," I said. "Khloe and I are really excited."

Clare smiled. "I can't wait. Movies. Junk food. Talking about boys. We need this after the first crazy week of school."

Riley surprised me by nodding. "Of course we'd be there," Riley said. "I'd be worried about Khloe if I wasn't there."

"Why would you be worried about Khloe?" I asked.

Riley made a sympathetic-slash-matter-of-fact face.

"She's going to be crushed after auditions. We'll get the cast list by tomorrow via e-mail and Khloe's going to need all the support she can get."

I clenched my jaw. I wasn't going to let Riley talk like that about Khloe. It was bad enough that she was doing it to Khloe's face, but she wasn't going to talk behind her back.

"Hey, let's go get warmed up," Clare said. Her voice was high and cheery. She looked back and forth between Riley and me.

"You're a wonderful actress," I said to Riley. She smiled as if I'd *finally* realized her talent.

"Thank y—"

I cut her off midword. "To pull it off that you're not worried about Khloe in auditions. I'm totally buying it, even though I know you're *way* smarter than to count Khloe out of snagging the lead."

I smiled sweetly and led Whisper away from Riley, Clare, Fuego, and Adonis.

I mounted, ignoring the dagger stares I felt Riley shooting at me. Lexa, who'd been walking Honor, rode up next to me.

"Why's Riley so mad at you?" Lexa whispered. "She looks like she's ready to knock you off Whisper!"

"She was trash-talking Khloe and I stood up to her," I said. "I tried to be nice because of the sleepover tonight, but Riley went after Khloe's acting and I couldn't keep my mouth closed."

Lex sighed. "She always has to start something. I'm glad you said whatever you did. Riley ran into us in the hallway today and told Khloe she was setting herself up for disappointment by even trying out for the lead. Riley said she didn't want Khloe getting hurt and to really consider trying out for a role she could realistically obtain."

I groaned. "That's the problem with Riley. She rarely ever says anything outright mean—it's always covered by this fake sugary sweetness."

"Lexa and Lauren," Mr. Conner's voice boomed across the arena, and I jumped in the saddle.

I looked over and Cole, Clare, Riley, and Drew were lined up in front of Mr. Conner. Lexa and I were walking our horses along the wall. I hadn't heard him come in!

Lex and I trotted Whisper and Honor to the end of the line. My cheeks blushed and I could barely look at Mr. Conner.

"Whatever conversation you two were having must have been extremely important," Mr. Conner said, crossing his arms.

"I'm sorry," Lexa and I said at the same time.

"So important," Mr. Conner said as if he hadn't heard us. "That if it wasn't the first week, I'd say you should continue it while you muck stalls after the lesson. This will be your first and last warning. Understood?"

"Yes, sir," I said.

Lexa nodded.

Stall duty was the *last* thing I wanted to do today before our sleepover. Lex and I had lucked out that Mr. Conner had given us a break. I wouldn't be caught not paying attention ever again.

"Please move your horses to the wall," Mr. Conner said.

Whisper and I ended up behind Cole and Valentino. I couldn't help but marvel at the lanky gelding's black coat. Not a spot on him had been bleached from the sun— every hair was a stunning, shiny black except for one white sock on his hind leg.

"Trot," Mr. Conner called.

All of my attention went to Whisper. This week's lesson was going to end on a good note.

Whisper stayed at a walk until I signaled her to trot. I posted, lifting myself slightly out of the saddle with the movement of her leg. She kept pace with the other horses

and there was an extra spring in her step. It was as if she knew it was Friday, too.

"Cross over the center, change direction, and sitting trot," Mr. Conner called.

Drew, at the front of the line, was the first to move over the arena's center. He'd put red bell boots on Polo and the blood bay trotted smoothly across the arena. The rest of us followed him.

We lapped the arena in the opposite direction and every muscle in Whisper's body was engaged. That was one of the most important qualities in a dressage horse. She had an ear back in my direction, listening.

"Canter," Mr. Conner called.

I deepened my seat, waiting for Whisper to react to the verbal cue. She didn't. Whisper kept a steady trot until I signaled her to canter. I smiled to myself. I couldn't wait to tell Khloe. She was going to be so happy.

Mr. Conner's eyes shifted from one of us to the other. He took notes, scribbling fast.

"Slow to a walk and bring your horses to the center, please," he said.

This time, Drew stopped Polo next to Whisper. He glanced over, smiling at me. I returned his smile, feeling my toes tingle. Drew was *très* cute. So cute. But I couldn't

start thinking about boys yet. Not right now. I had to learn how to juggle school, glee club, classes, friends, and everything else before I even *thought* about guys. But . . . that didn't mean I couldn't *look* at Drew.

I turned my gaze back to Mr. Conner.

"You all did well during your first week," he said. "On Monday, we'll begin more intensive work. I want you to rest up this weekend and prepare yourself. We're going to end the week's lessons with jumps."

Riley and Clare high-fived. Drew whispered, "Yes!"

I froze. What if I stayed like this—immobile—when it was my turn? It wasn't as if I could say *no.* I fidgeted with the reins. *You jumped all summer without a problem,* I reminded myself. *And you jumped during testing.* This felt different somehow. Maybe because I was riding in front of other people.

" . . . and then you'll be free to go," Mr. Conner said.

I caught the last few words of whatever he'd said.

Mike and Doug walked into the arena, carrying poles. Within minutes, they'd assembled three simple verticals in a straight line that increased in height.

"Drew, you'll go first," Mr. Conner said. "Followed by Lexa, Clare, Riley, Cole, and Lauren."

Being last was good and bad. It was good because I had

a chance to watch everyone else and bad because I had to wait which gave me more time to get nervous.

Everyone but Drew moved along the wall. He cantered Polo in a large circle then straightened him, pointing the horse at the first vertical. Polo rose into the air at the right second. His form, and Drew's, was near perfect. Drew eased Polo a notch and the two flew over the second vertical. They were magnetic—I couldn't take my eyes off them. Polo and Drew made a great team. Drew had gentle hands and he rode *with* Polo, not against him. They completed the last jump and Drew patted Polo's neck as he joined us.

"Nice work, Drew," Mr. Conner said.

I chewed the inside of my cheek as the rest of my team went. No one knocked a rail or even came close to a fault. I visualized all of the jumps Whisper and I had taken—and cleared—this summer. We could do this. Three simple verticals.

"Lauren, you're up," Mr. Conner said.

I eased Whisper forward the second he said my name. If I waited, I'd think too much. I didn't circle Whisper as some of my teammates had with their horses—I pointed her at the first vertical. All of the jumps were the same— white poles and black jump stands.

Whisper's canter was even as we approached the first vertical. I moved into the two-point position and gave Whisper rein. The gray mare stretched her neck, tucking her forelegs under her, and jumped into the air. We landed on the other side and I smiled.

I had to let Whisper be Whisper. I had to trust her. Sometimes, she responded to Mr. Conner's verbal cues. A few times, she'd balked at jumps over the summer, causing me more than a bruised ego. We didn't know each other well enough for me to let her wander like Khloe had with Ever. But Whisper trusted me. I owed her the same. It didn't mean I wasn't going to be nervous about jumping, but it *did* mean that I had to give Whisper room to try.

We cleared the second vertical and I gave her an extra inch of rein for the last jump. Whisper's body lifted into the air and she pushed off the ground with her hind legs, thrusting into the air. She landed and cantered away from the course. I rubbed her neck and she tossed her head, shaking her gray mane. Whisper knew she'd done well. There were lots of apple slices in her future.

I slowed her to a trot then a walk.

Mr. Conner nodded at me, giving me a quick smile. "Good ride, Lauren."

I couldn't stop a giant grin from spreading across my face.

"Thank you all, and I'll see you on Monday," Mr. Conner said.

I hopped off Whisper's back. "You were amazing, girl! I'm so proud of you. I couldn't have made it without you."

I looked over at Lexa as she dismounted. I wanted to share my excitement with her, but I couldn't. There wasn't anyone here that I could tell. Lexa and Khloe would wonder why I was so excited to have cleared three simple verticals.

I wanted to BBM Khloe before her lesson, so I led Whisper back to her stall to grab my phone.

Whisper didn't respond 2 any voice commands from Mr. C! Thank u so much!

Khloe is writing a message appeared.

I waited, glad I'd caught her before her class.

YAY! That's awesome, L! So happy 4 u! ☺ *Going 2 my lesson, but c u in r room.*

I put my phone back on my tack trunk and turned to Whisper.

"Okay, Princess Whisper, you're getting the royal treatment," I said. "Let's go to the wash stall."

Whisper *loved* water. She loved being pampered and often fell asleep when I bathed her.

I untacked her, leaving her gear on her stall door, and took her sky blue wash bucket, Mane 'n Tail shampoo and conditioner, a wide-toothed comb, and a sponge.

I led Whisper down the aisle, skipping the indoor wash stall and heading outside. The September sun wasn't as hot today. It peeked out from behind giant puffy clouds. The wash stall, on the stable's side, was free. The open space was as big as two box stalls and black rubber mats covered the concrete slab. A green hose was in a neat loop near the spigot.

I led Whisper inside and she turned around fast, standing ready for crossties. "Someone really wants a bath," I said, laughing.

I clipped the ties to her nylon halter and took off the lead rope. I hugged Whisper's neck and stared ahead of us. I squinted, looking at the cross-country field toward the woods at the back of the campus.

Mr. Conner stood near five mounted equestrians. A horse and rider I recognized soared over a tall brush jump and cantered to a double combination. The gorgeous bay took long strides and the rider's blond hair blew back. The separation between horse and rider was invisible.

Khloe and Ever.

Khloe slowed Ever, easing her just before they reached

the first half of the combination. The plastic poles, meant to look like logs, were probably about three and a half feet off the ground. I was too far away to be sure, but I'd had enough practice at eyeballing heights of obstacles.

Ever arched gracefully over the first jump, took one stride and lifted into the air for the second part of the combo. I didn't need to be close to see Khloe's excellent form. They circled and rode back to the waiting riders. I couldn't hear what Mr. Conner said to her, but it had to be good.

I smiled, squirting shampoo into the bucket and turning on the hose.

"We'll get there one day, girl," I told Whisper. "For now, we've got friends to cheer on."

I filled the bucket with warm water and suds threatened to overflow. I turned the hose to a gentle pressure and pointed it at Whisper's hooves. I worked my way up her legs, shoulder, neck, and by the time I reached her withers with the hose, her eyes closed.

The water ran over her hindquarters and down her tail, rinsing away a week of lessons, dust, and sweat.

Once her soaked coat darkened, I turned off the hose and started soaping her left foreleg from hoof, to knee, to forearm. Whisper's eyes remained shut as bubbles covered

her body and I scrubbed her coat in a circular motion. I paid extra attention to her girth, withers, and back— places where she'd gathered the most sweat.

After she was clean, I rinsed her coat and massaged conditioner into it. Whisper went in and out of sleep throughout the bath and her calm demeanor relaxed me. Moments like these made me fall in love with her even more.

33

BREAK A LEG

"'PLEASE, GASTON. I CAN'T. I HAVE TO GET home and help my father,'" Khloe said. "Ugh! I'm not using that. I'm going back to my first choice. That was awful, wasn't it?"

"No, it wasn't," I said. "Khlo, you *know* every word of your monologues—whatever one you choose. You *are* Belle."

Khloe looked up at the media center entrance and took a huge breath. We'd been standing outside for several minutes while Khloe rehearsed parts of her monologue. She looked great in a blue tissue T-shirt that matched the color of Belle's dress, dark skinny jeans, and black ballet flats. She'd flatironed her hair and had applied a little more makeup than usual.

"You're such a good friend," Khloe said. "Okay. I'm going with my first choice. I'm ready."

We walked inside the media center and I stopped at the theater entrance. Khloe peeked inside to see if anyone was watching the door. I wanted to see her audition and be there for support like she'd done for me and glee club.

Khloe reached over and tugged my hand. "C'mon! Hurry!" I tiptoed after her through the door.

We passed an older girl with gorgeous cat-eye makeup who winked at us and didn't say a word.

"Jana assists Mr. Barber," Khloe whispered. "I asked her if I could sneak you in and she said just this once."

The stage was empty—the spotlight waiting for its next audition.

Khloe took me to a back row of seats and pointed to one at the end. "Sit there and stay still. Duck if you see anyone coming."

"Okay," I said. "I won't get caught. Promise. When do you go on?"

"Jana said to go wait backstage. There's one person ahead of me then I'm up."

I hugged Khloe. "Break a leg!"

"Thanks for being here," Khloe said. "It means a lot." With a smile, she disappeared and headed backstage.

I sat in the dark, glad no one could see my face. Khloe was so grateful that I was here for her, but I felt like a fraud. She didn't know Lauren Towers. She only knew the Lauren that I'd introduced her to. I'd kept her at arm's length—letting her in, but not too much. There hadn't been one conversation where I hadn't been waiting for it. With Khloe's status in dressage at Canterwood, I was almost positive she'd recognize my name. So far, she'd gotten to know *me*, but not all of me.

That's it, I decided. *I'm telling her after the sleepover.*

"May I have the next person?" Mr. Barber asked.

My attention went to the stage as a girl emerged from the wings and stepped into the spotlight.

Riley. She'd curled her hair into soft waves, had pink glossy lips, and mascara that made her eyes pop even from my faraway seat. Like Khloe, she'd dressed in Belle's blue, only she wore a casual-slash-preppy blue dress with capped sleeves. She'd paired the dress with wedges.

"Hello," she said. Her voice, clear and strong but not too loud, reached me in the back row. She addressed a teacher sitting at a banquet table with a desk light on, who I'd assumed was Mr. Barber.

"My name is Riley Edwards. I'm auditioning for the role of Belle."

"Do you have a monologue prepared?" Mr. Barber asked.

"Yes, sir," Riley said. "I have one that's a minute long and another that's two. I'll perform whichever you like."

I hated to admit it, even to myself, but Riley looked and sounded great onstage. She hadn't even delivered her monologue yet.

"One minute is perfect," Mr. Barber said. "Thank you for having two options. I appreciate it."

Riley smiled, bowing her head. It was the smile she saved for adults—one that made her seem angelic.

Riley kept her head down, then looked up. She walked to the edge of the stage.

"'Little town, it's a quiet village,'" she sang. She started back across the stage and even without props or scenery, I visualized her walking through a town.

Uh-oh. Riley was fantastic. Her voice, presence, and look mesmerized me. If she did this without a costume, other actors, props or scenery, I couldn't even imagine . . .

"'Every day like the one before. Little town, full of . . .'"

Riley sang for minute, but it felt like seconds. I wanted to be bored, but I couldn't look away. Her beautiful singing voice hit every note and she finished with a smile.

"Thank you, Riley," Mr. Barber said. "You will be informed of my decision via e-mail tomorrow."

"Thank you, sir," Riley said. She exited the stage, disappearing behind the curtain.

Mr. Barber kept his head bent over his desk for a few minutes, probably taking notes on her performance.

Jana walked over to him, showing him the sign-in sheet.

"Next!" Mr. Barber called.

Khloe walked out from behind the blue velvet curtains and stopped in the spotlight.

"I'm Khloe Kinsella. I've prepared a monologue for the role of Belle."

Khloe's voice had a slight wobble to it. I gripped the armrests. *Shake it off,* I thought, trying to send a message via ESP to Khloe. I hoped Riley hadn't said something to rattle her. But I had to give Khloe more credit. She was an actress. It was a cutthroat business and she'd probably encountered a dozen Rileys at auditions.

Like Riley, Khloe had chosen to sing for her audition. In this monologue, Belle was supposed to be singing to a chicken and to her horse.

Khloe reached into her pocket, pulled out an imaginary handful of something and began scattering it like she was feeding chickens. She crouched down, holding out a hand.

"'Is he gone? Can you imagine, he asked me to marry him! Me, the wife . . .'"

All of the nerves had disappeared from Khloe's voice. Just like with Riley, I could see the setting in my head as she delivered her lines. Khloe sang with a stunning, sweet voice that gave me chills. I'd see my roommate on Broadway one day—I knew it.

Khloe wrapped up her audition and looked at Mr. Barber. I had to hold myself back from cheering—she'd *nailed* it! Khloe had been perfect. But so had Riley.

"Khloe, thank you," Mr. Barber said. "You'll have the casting list in your inbox tomorrow morning."

"Thank you, Mr. Barber." Khloe left the stage and I sneaked out of the auditorium to meet her in the media center.

Khloe came down a side hallway and I clasped my hands together when I saw her.

"You were *très magnifique!*" I said. "I didn't see Khloe Kinsella. I saw Belle on her farm. You hit every note. I'm so proud of you!"

Khloe grinned. "Thanks, Laur. I'm sooo glad it's over! Now we can enjoy the sleepover and have fun tonight."

We left the media center, walking back toward Hawthorne.

"Do you agonize over the wait?" I asked. "Or will the sleepover distract you?"

"Actually, I stopped obsessing about whether or not I got cast for roles a while ago. I realized that after my audition, I'd done my job. The casting director either thought I was right for the part or didn't. As long as I give my best onstage, I don't really worry."

"That's great. It means you're going to have a really awesome time tonight! Now I can save all of the things I'd thought up to distract you for when they're needed."

Khloe and I laughed together as we entered Hawthorne. It was time to get our room ready. People would be at our door in less than a couple of hours. I couldn't wait to get the evening started!

34
TRUTH OR DARE?

"YAY! YOU'RE HERE!" KHLOE SAID, OPENING our door. Lexa and Jill, sleeping bags and overnight satchels in hand, arrived first.

"Thanks for inviting us," Lex said.

Jill put her hot-pink sleeping bag with black stars out of the way next to the wall. "Yeah, thanks so much. Every time I thought my brains were going to explode during class, I pictured tonight."

"Same," I said. "Now I've officially survived my first week at Canterwood."

Lexa high-fived me. "You're definitely a Canterwood student now. Enjoy *every* second of this weekend because it's like the teachers make it their personal mission to give us as much work as possible. They think they let us 'take it easy' the first week."

Jill groaned, taking off her glasses to rub her eyes. "Please don't even say the words 'teachers' or 'work.'"

The three of us laughed until someone knocked on the door. Lexa's eyes met mine. She didn't get along with Riley, but tried to for Khloe's sake.

I opened the door this time. "Hey," I said, smiling at Clare and Riley. Both girls were dressed like the rest of us—in loungy pants and T-shirts.

"Hi," Clare said. "TGIF!"

"Seriously," I said. "C'mon in."

Riley didn't say a word as she stepped through the doorway. I sighed to myself. I wasn't going to let her drag down the night. Khloe and I had made a pact to include her in everything and not to engage her if she tried to start an argument.

Clare said hi to the other girls and put her stuff with everyone else's. Riley's eyes went over every inch of our room.

"Nice color choices," Riley said.

Everyone paused. Did I hear her right? I waited for a "but . . ." to follow. Riley didn't say anything else.

"Thanks," Khloe said. "Lauren and I used our favorite colors and, luckily, they matched."

We all traded a bit more small talk and everyone seemed to relax by the minute. Even Riley. I wondered if she'd been nervous about the sleepover.

"Want to change into pj's and decide what to do first?" I asked.

Everyone agreed and we took turns changing in the bathroom. We ended up sitting or lying in different places in the room. Riley and Clare were on their stomachs on Khloe's bed, Lexa and I sprawled on our sides on the rug, and Jill and Khloe sat on my bed.

"I love our pajamas," I said. "We look like we could be in a commercial or something."

"So true," Jill said. She ran a hand through her brown hair, giving it volume and making a face as if she was looking into a camera.

We all giggled. Our pj's really were cool—everyone had colorful pants or shorts paired with tank tops. I'd chosen a hot-pink tank with white stitching and white shorts. Khloe had dressed in her favorite color. She wore a spaghetti strap yellow tank top with white polka dots and matching shorts with ruffled hems.

I was glad Khloe and I had stocked up on various sodas. Almost everyone was drinking something different. Clare sipped grape, Riley had diet root beer, Jill and Lexa drank

Sprites, I had cherry Diet Pepsi, and Khloe had already finished her Mountain Dew. I'd offered everyone a choice of a different crazy straw and even Riley couldn't help but smile when she'd picked a red swirly one.

"So, you actually think Hailey is going out with Jason?" Clare asked.

"Yes!" Jill said, nodding so hard she shook the bed. "They're totally keeping it on the DL 'cause Hailey is only dating Jason to get back at Brad."

"Oh, stop," Riley interjected, but not in a mean way. We'd been gossiping and giggling for a while. Khloe had set bowls of M&M's, popcorn, chips, and pretzels on the coffee table though the food had been forgotten when the talking had started. The TV was on low in the background, set on our agreed-upon favorite reality TV network—Watch!—but no one was paying attention.

"It's true," Lex said. She pulled her curls into a high ponytail. "I heard Hailey in the bathroom the other day. She told Kacie that Jason wasn't even a six, but he was perfect because he's Brad's biggest competition on the basketball team."

"Ouch," I said. "That's harsh."

I'd been having so much fun listening to everyone and learning the scandals at school.

"No kidding," Khloe said. "Jayllex told me that Brad's so jealous, he's going to blow it at the next game if he doesn't cool it."

I got up, realizing I'd forgotten some of the candy. I dug through a box in my closet and found the bags of Japanese candy that I'd ordered online for tonight. Becca, crazy about manga and anime, had spent a lot of free time watching Japanese cartoons over the summer. She'd discovered a store full of Asian candy when we'd made a trip back to New York City and, thankfully for Becs, the store had a website. She'd used a lot of her allowance on the candy and had gotten me hooked.

I set the bags on the table and everyone stopped talking, staring at the bags. I'd gotten Meiji Yan Yan sticks with strawberry crème and chocolate hazelnut dip, Hello Kitty sour gummies, and an assortment of Haribo fruit-flavored gummies.

"What kind of candy is that?" Riley asked, her nose wrinkled but her eyes curious.

"It's Japanese candy," I explained. "My sister got me addicted to it over the summer."

Clare got off the bed and knelt by the coffee table. She picked up a packet of strawberry Pocky Sticks and turned them over in her hands. "Oooh. These look good."

"Where'd you get it?" Lexa asked. Like Clare, she got beside the table.

"I ordered it online. My mom took my sister and me back to Brooklyn this summer to visit our friends and we went into Manhattan. Becca found this candy shop and almost bought everything in the store."

"You used to live in *Brooklyn*?" Jill asked. She straightened her glasses. "What was it like?"

Khloe ripped open a bag of Hello Kitty sours. Lexa took a couple and tossed one to Riley. I opened my favorite and Becca's—Kasugai kiwi gummies. I loved that the candies even had kiwi seeds inside.

"I loved Brooklyn," I said. "It was eclectic and laid-back. I liked that I had access to the city, but didn't live in Manhattan. It's fun to visit, but too busy for me."

"Manhattan's just like Canterwood," Riley said. "You have to keep up or you'll get run over."

No one said anything to that. We munched on candy and watched TV. Riley's phone rang. An odd look flashed on her face. Riley fumbled for her BlackBerry, silencing the ringer. Everyone else's phones were away, but Riley had kept hers out. She was probably waiting for things to get boring so she could text or play on her phone.

Riley stood, smoothing her white tank with a glittery

black heart. "Be back in a sec." She took her phone, skirted around the coffee table and went out into the hallway, closing the door behind her.

"Okaaay," Lexa said. "She can't talk in here?"

Clare picked up a peach candy. "I think it's an ex or someone from home. She always leaves our room, too, when she gets calls like that."

"You're her friend and she won't even tell you?" Jill asked.

"Nope. I asked once and, believe me, I'll never ask again," Clare said.

The door opened and Riley stepped back inside. Her cheeks were a little flushed. Clare was probably right— maybe Riley had been talking to an ex. Or a secret boyfriend back home.

The rest of us pretended like we'd been absorbed in TV while Riley had been on the phone.

"Want to order pizza?" I asked.

"And watch a movie when it comes?" Khloe added.

Everyone nodded. Khloe dialed The Slice and placed our order.

Riley looked at us with a gleam in her brown eyes. "This *is* a sleepover. We *have* to play truth or dare!"

That sounded dangerous. Playing truth or dare would

be fun with the other girls, but not with Riley. Somehow, she was going to ask the wrong question or dare someone to do something awful.

"Um . . . ," I said, looking at Khloe for help.

She looked back, wide-eyed. "Yeah, maybe we—"

"I'll start," Riley said, cutting Khloe off and not waiting for an answer if anyone else wanted to play.

"Fine, but we *have* to keep the dares contained to the room," Khloe said, her voice firm. "We'll never be allowed to have another sleepover again if Christina finds out we left."

"Deal," Clare said. The rest of us nodded. Except for Riley.

"Riley?" Khloe asked.

Riley waved her hand. "Yeah, deal. Whatever." Riley took her time looking at each of us. "Lexa," she finally said. "Truth or dare?"

"Truth," Lexa said.

"Who was your first kiss?" Riley asked.

Lexa traced the pink stripe that ran down her pant leg. She stared at Riley, her head up. "I haven't kissed a boy yet."

Riley smirked then frowned. "That was so rude of me. I'm so sorry for you, Lex. It's not fun to be, like, the only girl in our grade not to have been kissed."

"I'm totally cool with it, *Riley*," Lexa said, almost spitting out Riley's name. "I'm not going to kiss any random guy just to say I've been kissed."

"Your turn, Lex," Jill interjected.

Lexa glared at Riley. I was *sure* she'd pick Riley and retaliate. "Khloe," Lexa said.

Major relief. I should have known that Lexa was more mature than Riley.

"Dare," Khloe said, grinning.

Lexa thought for a moment. "Got it. Take a picture of yourself in a silly pose, scroll through your address book with your eyes closed, stop, and send it to the name you land on."

"Do it, do it!" I said, laughing.

"Omigod," Khloe said. "What if I send it to a guy or something?"

Lexa giggled. "Let's hope not."

Khloe, being a good sport, grabbed her phone. She turned it around and pointed the camera at her face. She stuck out her tongue, crossed her eyes, and the flash went off.

Everyone, even Riley, laughed.

"Now scroll," Lexa said.

Khloe held the phone away from her, closed her eyes,

and scanned her address book. She thrust the phone at Jill. "Tell me who it is! I can't look."

Jill stared at Khloe's screen. "This. Is. So. Perfect!" She handed it back to Khloe and all of our eyes followed the phone.

Through squinted eyes, Khloe peeked. "Nooo!" Her face reddened and she slapped a hand over her forehead.

"Who is it?" Lexa asked.

"Tell!" I said.

Khloe lowered her head. "It's . . . Zack."

"Zack, as in the Zack that you and Lex were freaking out over when he talked to me on Monday?" I asked.

"Yes," Khloe mumbled. She held the phone facedown.

"Why do you have Zack's number?" Riley asked.

"Because we're science partners," Khloe said.

"Doesn't matter!" Clare said. "Send it."

"Guys . . ." Khloe made puppy eyes at us.

"We're waiting," Lexa said, smiling.

Khloe rolled her eyes then pressed a couple of buttons on her phone. "Zack's going to think I'm so weird for sending him this. It'll ruin my reputation forever with boys here and I won't ever go on a date, I'll end up going to senior prom alone and—"

"Senior prom?" I asked, giggling. "If we have to,

we'll worry about getting you a date for *seventh* grade, okay?"

Khloe held out the phone, a check mark next to the photo and Zack's name. "There. Thanks, Lex." She tossed a Hello Kitty gummy at her friend.

"My turn," Khloe said. "Lauren. Truth or dare?"

"Truth," I said, eating a pretzel stick.

"If your ex came to campus, would you date him or keep your options open?" Khloe asked.

"Ex?" Clare asked. "I didn't know you had an ex! Why you did you break up? I so need details!"

Khloe glanced at me. "We're playing truth or dare, Clare, not spill your guts. Ask Laur later."

I'd thank Khloe later for saving me from retelling my Taylor story.

"If he came to Canterwood," I said. "I don't know what I'd do, honestly. It's only my first week here and I'm not looking for guys, but there are definitely some hot ones."

"Okay," Khloe said. She tugged at the end of her French braid. "Your turn."

"Riley," I said.

Riley tossed a few M&M's into her mouth. "Dare."

Exactly what I'd been hoping for. Clare may have been too scared to ask about Riley's mystery caller, but I wasn't. I thought about the day I'd heard her in the stable and how there wasn't any other possible question to ask.

"Show us the last call on your phone," I said. "The one who just called. I want to know who your mystery person is."

Riley's hand went to her phone, clutching it. She locked eyes with me—like she could scare me into taking it back.

"Riles!" Clare said. "Omigod, I *thought* you had a secret boyfriend, but now I'm totally sure!"

"Clare," Riley's tone was warning.

"Is he someone we both liked and that's why you didn't tell me?" Clare continued.

"Show us, Riley," Jill said. "The game was your idea."

With a cool look, Riley played with her phone and handed it to me.

"There," she said.

"Toby," I read aloud, handing her back the phone.

"Toby?" Jill said as she, Lexa, Clare, and Khloe looked at each other.

"I can't think of one guy in our class named Toby," Khloe said. "Oooh, is he older? Like, in eighth grade or high school?"

Riley pressed her lips together. I'd never seen her like

this. Something was off. Why wouldn't she say who it was?

Clare elbowed her best friend. "I'm your BFF. Tell me. We all promise," Clare looked at each of us. "not to tell *anyone* outside of this room."

"It's okay, Riley," I said, using the patronizing tone she'd perfected. "You don't have to share anything. I mean, there must be a good reason why you want to keep Toby a secret."

"Yeah," Lexa said. "If he *is* your secret boyfriend—"

"He's not my boyfriend!" Riley yelled.

We stared at her, afraid to move. I don't think anyone was breathing. Riley's outburst had silenced the room. Even the TV seemed quieter.

"Never mind," Clare said quietly. "You don't have to tell."

"No, you all want to know *so* bad," Riley's voice hovered a notch below yelling. "I'll tell you exactly who Toby is. I *love* Toby so much."

So he was her . . .

"Toby is my little brother. He has Down syndrome. Those secret phone calls to my 'boyfriend' were to my parents about my brother. Or my brother calling me."

Oh, my God. This was all my fault.

"Riley, I'm so sorry," I said. "You don't have to say anything else. We never should have pushed you. I'm sorry I asked the question."

A tear ran down Riley's face and she swiped it away with her hand. "You know who's sorry, Lauren? *I* am. You know who should be the one apologizing? I should. To my brother."

Clare eased next to Riley and, tentatively, put an arm across her shoulders. Riley didn't shrug Clare off.

"When I left my old school to come to Canterwood, I also left Toby," Riley continued. It was as if she couldn't stop talking. Like she needed to tell someone. Like the secret had been too much to hide alone. I empathized with her more than she knew.

"Last year, my mom called and said Toby was being teased by some kids in his class," Riley said, more tears falling. "It was my fault. I'd always been there to protect him from those *stupid* kids who didn't understand. I told Mom that I wanted to come home, but she said no. Toby wouldn't want me to."

"I bet your mom was right," Khloe said, her voice soft. The rest of us nodded.

"I went home last summer and spent tons of time with Toby. We went to the arcade, bowled, and I took him to

the water park. I don't care if it sounds lame, but he's fun to be with and he's my friend, too."

"It's not lame," I said. "My sister is one of my best friends. Toby sounds like a special kid."

Riley smiled. "He is. He has friends at school, gets awesome grades, and loves baseball. This year, he entered fifth grade. At first, my mom kept telling me that everything was fine with him. My dad said the same thing. And Toby . . . he was so cheerful and happy just to talk to me every time I called."

No one interrupted. Riley needed this. I was embarrassed that I'd eavesdropped on her at the stable. The conversation had obviously been about Toby.

"Finally, my mom told me the truth. She said the teasing had escalated. Toby came home crying more than once. That wouldn't have happened if I'd been there. If I still lived at home, I'd be at the same school as Toby and even if I hadn't been there when those jerks teased him, I would have been there to comfort him."

Riley sniffled and Clare handed her another tissue.

"You're a good big sister," Jill said. "He'll always see you as his protector. I bet Toby wouldn't want you to give up your dream. I can't imagine how you must feel, being here and knowing what he's going through."

"You're talking to him," Lexa said. "You guys should Skype—I bet he'd loved that."

Lexa's suggestion made Riley smile. "He would. I don't know why I didn't think of that."

I hesitated, wondering if I should ask. "How is Toby? Is everything okay?"

Riley nodded. "Everything's great, actually. I always assume something's wrong when he calls, but he wanted to tell me that he was having a sleepover tonight with two boys in his class."

"That's awesome," I said.

"So cool," Lexa said. "Did you tell him that his big sis was at a sleepover, too?"

"I did," Riley said. "I told him we were going to watch a girly movie and he said 'eww' and laughed a lot."

Someone knocked at the door and Khloe jumped up to open it.

"Pizza, anyone?" Christina asked, holding our delivery.

"Thank you," Khloe said. "Want a slice?"

"You know what? Sure," Christina said. "That's really sweet."

Christina picked out a piece of pepperoni pizza and a napkin. "Have fun, girls," she said as she left.

I passed out purple paper plates and matching napkins.

We all took slices of pizza and no one made a move to start the movie. Instead, we fell into a conversation about our families. Jill lightened the mood by sharing a hilarious story about a family vacay gone seriously wrong when her dad, deciding to go GPS free, had driven one hundred miles in the *wrong* direction on a trip to the Smokey Mountains. Khloe talked about her twin sisters and how they always pulled the switching act on her.

By 2:00 a.m., the game of truth or dare seemed long forgotten. Colorful sleeping bags were spread all over the floor and we were losing the fight to stay awake.

Riley, Clare, and Jill were already snuggled into their sleeping bags.

"G'night," Khloe said to Lexa.

"Night, guys," Lexa whispered, her voice heavy with sleep.

I slipped under my cool covers and Khloe hit the light, bathing the room in darkness.

35
REALITY LT

"GUYS, WAKE UP! OMIGOD!"

I sat up, my heart pounding. "What's wrong?" I asked, my vision fuzzy. It was just after eight.

Riley stood next to her sleeping bag, clutching her phone to her chest. Lexa, Jill, and Clare sat up in their sleeping bags, blinking and rubbing their eyes.

"Nothing's wrong!" Riley said. She seemed like she'd already had five cups of coffee. "The casting e-mail went out!"

That woke Khloe up. "*What*? It's out? Like, *now* now?" Khloe reached for her phone.

I gripped my covers, nervous *for* Khloe. Either Riley *didn't* get the lead and she was acting cool, pretending she never wanted it, or . . .

Khloe stared at her screen for a second before putting the phone on her desk. She looked at Riley and smiled.

I knew that smile.

She didn't get it.

"Congratulations," Khloe said, smiling at Riley with admirable grace. "You'll make a great Belle."

"I know! I worked *so* hard for that part. Oh—I know you did your best, Khloe. And I'm sure you'll make a great Mrs. Potts—she has a lot of lines."

Riley, however, could have learned a thing or twelve about grace—*from* Khloe.

"Thanks," Khloe said. "I really do love that character."

"Me too," I piped up. "We're going to have the *best* time running lines together." I flashed her a smile, making sure that it was a *Yay, fun!* smile, rather than a *you poor thing—maybe it'll feel better later* smile.

"And don't even worry about that weird, heavy costume," Riley said. "Maybe you can do strength training before opening night."

And on that note . . .

"Congratulations to *both* of you," I said. "I love *Beauty and the Beast*. I can't wait to see you onstage."

Riley, Clare, Jill, and Lex congratulated Riley and Khloe. I caught Khloe's eye and she did *not* look happy.

I didn't want to stay in the room any longer and give Riley a chance to brag about being Belle. Khloe needed a distraction.

"I'm *starving*," I said. "Anybody interested in staying in our pj's, having breakfast in the common room, and watching something awesome on TV?"

"I'm in," Clare said.

Everyone started to get up, stretching, brushing hair, re-doing ponytails.

Riley had an annoying perma-gloat about her.

Khloe acted as cheerful as she'd been last night, but when she turned away from the group, her eyes were downcast. Khloe had worked so hard. She deserved to play Belle.

"Since we have two very talented actresses in our midst," I said. "Who were just cast in huge roles in the musical . . . I think we should get dessert with breakfast. Anyone else in?"

"Hmmm, let me think . . . ," Lexa said, grinning. "Hello, ice cream sundae!"

Clare nodded, putting on fuzzy orange slippers. "I wouldn't *hate* starting Saturday morning with a brownie."

Khloe shot me a real smile. "Dessert sounds perfect. Good idea, LT."

"I think we should spring for Riley's and Khloe's

desserts," Jill said. "One condition, when you're both famous and making millions, both of you'll remember this moment and send me killer presents."

Riley and Khloe laughed.

"Aaand," Jill continued. "I was thinking . . . I don't know much about horses and you're *all* riders. Should we watch a horse show DVD or something? Maybe I'll learn a thing or two."

Jill was being a great friend to Khloe by helping to cheer her up.

"Oh, Jill," Khloe said, slinging an arm across the girl's shoulder. "You never should have opened that door. We might subject you to an entire *morning* of horse shows."

The second we started out the door, someone's phone rang.

"That's mine," I said, heading toward my nightstand. "It's my mom. If I don't get it, she'll worry. You guys go ahead and start the DVD. I'll be right there!"

The girls nodded, closing the door behind them.

"Hi, Mom," I answered.

"Hi, honey. How's your Saturday?"

I sat at the end of my bed. "Great. Khloe and I had a sleepover last night. We're about to have breakfast and watch a DVD."

"Sounds fun!" Mom said. "Oh, sweetie, I'm glad you're making friends. You always do, don't you? No matter where you are."

"What are you, Dad, and Becs doing?" I asked.

"The usual," Mom said. "Dad's on the porch with coffee and the paper, I doubt we'll see Becca before noon, and I've got some paperwork to catch up on."

"Sounds like a really nice morning," I said.

Saturday mornings *were* good at home. I could picture everything Mom had described. It made me suddenly feel very homesick just thinking about the fact that I wasn't going to float in the pool with Becca this afternoon, or beg Dad to take me to the stable—or even ask Mom for a PB&J.

The longer we talked, the better I felt, though. Maybe I wasn't going to have *those* things this weekend, but I had my new friends waiting for me. Maybe we'd start our own weekend traditions.

Mom and I talked for a few more minutes before hanging up.

I hurried out to the common room, ready to rejoin everyone and order breakfast. Waffles with whipped cream sounded better by the second.

"That was *so* fun!" I heard Jill say as I neared the room. "I've *never* seen jumping like that."

"It's a clean ride for Eve Ortiz," an announcer said.

Eve Ortiz. Why does that name sound so familiar?

I walked into the common room. Everyone was gathered around the TV.

"Sorry about that," I said. "What DVD did you guys—"

"Up next in cross-country is two-time junior dressage champion, Lauren Towers," the announcer called. The camera panned to me and Skyblue. I was dressed in my best navy coat, white shirt, stock tie, spotless breeches, and shiny boots. But I didn't have to see the footage to remember what I'd worn on that particular day.

This could *not* be happening.

I rested my back against the wall for support and let my body slide down.

"Omigod, it's *you!*" Jill said, turning to look at me. "I just picked a random DVD and *you're* in it?! You were on TV! You're, like, famous!"

More like infamous, I thought, holding my head.

I was completely frozen. I couldn't move. Or breathe.

I knew I had to stop the DVD, but all I could do was stare at my "new friends."

Everyone was about to see my accident and find out the secret I'd been trying to keep for almost two years. I was an *ex*-champion with confidence issues.

Nausea washed over me, making me woozy. I hadn't wanted *Khloe* to find out this way. And I'd only just been hours away from telling her the truth.

"LT?" Khloe said, softly.

"*Khloe,*" I said.

"You never told me you were a dressage champion!" Lexa said, excitedly. "How come? That's your favorite discipline!"

Riley didn't say a word. I watched as she sat there, expressionless, taking it all in.

"Guys, that's not *our* LT!" Khloe said. "Okay, so they look a lot alike, but that's *not* Whisper."

TV-Lauren cued Skyblue into a canter and cleared the first brush jump. I didn't need to look at the screen to remember the exact course.

Each girl kept shifting her gaze from the screen to me. But all I could do was stay along the wall, quiet.

"They're approaching the final jump," the announcer said, his voice getting louder. "Lauren's ride is clean and her time is fastest. She is our final competitor. If Lauren and Skyblue clear this jump, they've clinched first place— and a *huge* win for Double Aces."

"Lauren? Come sit with us!" Jill patted the seat next to her, but I didn't move.

I closed my eyes.

This was when everything had gone horribly, horribly wrong. Somehow, I tuned out the sounds of hooves skidding on grass, a body hitting the ground, and a giant, gasping crowd.

"Oh, my God," Riley whispered.

Then I opened my eyes. Riley, Clare, Lexa, Jill, and Khloe were all staring at me.

Without breaking her stare, Khloe paused the DVD.

"Lauren," Khloe said, too slow. "Was that you?"

I looked directly into my roommate's eyes. And suddenly, I knew I had to say it.

"No," I said, vehement. "The person on TV is *not* me."

ABOUT THE AUTHOR

Twenty-four-year-old Jess Burkhart (a.k.a. Jess Ashley) writes from Brooklyn, New York. She's obsessed with sparkly things, lip gloss, and TV. She loves hanging with her bestie, watching too much TV, and shopping for all things Hello Kitty. Learn more about Jess at www.jessicaburkhart.com. Find everything Canterwood Crest at www.canterwoodcrest.com.

Real life. Real you.

Don't miss
any of these
terrific
Aladdin M!X
books.

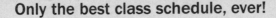